CARLA'S REVENGE

Society girl Carla Bowman is young, beautiful — and wild. She is the honey of King Logan, a gangster running a protection racket on New York's East Side, and she becomes caught up in violence and bloodshed. Carla double-crosses Logan and joins his rival, Sylvester Shapirro, only to become his captive in a sanatorium. She escapes, but when she learns that Shapirro has killed her father, Carla's only desire is to revenge her father's death — whatever the cost to herself . . .

SYDNEY J. BOUNDS

CARLA'S REVENGE

Complete and Unabridged

LINFORD
Leicester

First published in Great Britain

First Linford Edition
published 2008

The moral right of the author has been asserted

British Library CIP Data

Bounds, Sydney J.
    Carla's revenge.—Large print ed.—
Linford mystery library
    1. Organized crime—New York (State)—
New York—Fiction 2. Detective and mystery
stories 3. Large type books
    I. Title
823.9'14 [F]

ISBN 978–1–84782–490–5

Published by
F. A. Thorpe (Publishing)
Anstey, Leicestershire

Set by Words & Graphics Ltd.
Anstey, Leicestershire
Printed and bound in Great Britain by
T. J. International Ltd., Padstow, Cornwall

This book is printed on acid-free paper

1

The car was a Lincoln. It was wide as a tank, and streamlined; the nose was curved, the tail narrowing to a cigar-shape. The steel plates had been reinforced, painted a drab olive-green, and the windows were curved and bulletproof. It was not the sort of car an honest citizen would need in his daily chores.

The car sped through the narrow dimly-lit streets of Manhattan's East Side and turned into the Bowery. It stopped outside a dingy shop with boarded windows. The sign over the door was old, the paintwork flaked, but the words were still legible:

JOE MAZZINI
Coffins To Order

Two men and a girl got out of the olive-green Lincoln and walked across to the shop. The girl was very young and very beautiful, and she looked as out of place in the Bowery as a mouse in a cat's home. But appearances can be deceptive.

She had raven-black hair, short and bobbed, an oval face that was smooth and dark complexioned, wide eyes with jet-black pupils, and perfectly shaped lips brightly coloured with crimson lipstick.

The evening gown she wore was whiter than snow and didn't need shoulder straps for support, not in the way it conformed to the mature curvature of her figure. The gown flattered her slim waist and tapering hips, dropping about her ankles. She had high-heeled shoes that sparkled diamonds, and sheer silk hose. She might have been anywhere from nineteen to twenty-one and she had the beauty of youth and maturity combined.

For an instant, she passed through the bright beam of the Lincoln's headlamps and the white dress hung like a pellucid net about her, revealing slender limbs, and curves of grace and beauty.

Her bare shoulders were dark-skinned, half-covered by a white fur wrap, and she carried a tiny handbag of black leather.

The way she walked, swaying from the hips, and the eager light in her jet-black eyes, revealed a suppressed excitement. She wasn't tall, but what there was of her was just as perfect as a woman can be.

Her two companions would have passed as typical Bowery thugs. One was broad and heavy, slow of movement and thinking. He wasn't particular about his dress and wore brown shoes with a blue suit. His face was wrinkled and scarred, his nose flattened and his eyes dull. He looked capable of carrying out simple orders, if they were spelled out in words of a single syllable.

The other man dressed flashily. His royal blue tie clashed with a beige shirt, which clashed in turn with a fawn jacket with wide lapels and razor-creased slacks of bright green. His face was lean and hard and shadowed by the brim of a Fedora hat. He was no taller than the girl but he swaggered as if he knew how smart he was.

All three went into the shop on Nugget Street in New York's Bowery. A passage led to a workshop littered with planks of wood, joiner's tools, and half-completed coffins. There were shavings on the floor, and an unpleasant smell in the air.

The girl's nose didn't wrinkle at the smell; she might have been used to death.

'Hi, Joe,' she said in a soft drawl. 'This is a business call.'

Joe Mazzini laid down a chisel and looked up. He didn't look as if he were pleased by the call. He was thin and bony with a grey face and a twitch about his mouth. His feet shifted almost as much as his watery eyes.

'Wotcher want?' he said, looking from the girl to her two companions. He seemed more than a little uneasy about something.

The girl held out an immaculately manicured hand. Her nails were crimson to match her lips.

'Five hundred bucks,' she said casually.

Joe looked down at the floor and scuffed wood-shavings with his foot. His twitch was giving him trouble.

'I can't pay it, Carla,' he mumbled. He had to moisten his lips before he could go on. 'I can't pay any more.'

Carla smiled bleakly. Her jet-black pupils contracted to pinpoints as she looked at Joe Mazzini. She loosened the fur wrap about her throat and leaned on a coffin.

'Warm in here,' she drawled. 'Shouldn't be surprised if you had a fire one day, Joe. All this wood — make a swell bonfire. Now, for five hundred bucks, you get protection against fire. A sort of insurance policy.'

'I can't pay,' said Joe Mazzini, 'not any longer.'

Carla frowned, and how she managed to do it without looking any less beautiful is just one of those things.

'Why not, Joe?' she asked softly. 'You're doing good business. Why, we've put some business your way ourselves.'

She glanced at the unfinished coffin.

'Old Rory,' she said, nodding towards the coffin. 'He stopped paying insurance — then a car knocked him down. His relatives are paying for the coffin, aren't they?'

'It's not that,' Joe mumbled. 'I'm paying insurance to another outfit, these days.'

There was a sudden hush. It hung over the room like midnight over a graveyard. Then the flashily-dressed man began to swear. The words he used would have made an innocent girl blush — Carla heard him out without blinking an eyelid, then said:

'Looks like you'll have to convince him there's only one *sound* insurance company in the Bowery, Nick.'

Nick tipped back his Fedora and smiled coldly. He took a step forward, slowly, as if he had all the time in the world. It was then that a new voice said:

'I wouldn't bother.'

Nick stopped as if he'd trodden on a rattlesnake. Carla turned to see a man come through the door at the rear of the shop. He was strikingly handsome and quietly dressed in a grey lounge suit. His hair was blond, his eyes blue, and he sauntered forward with confident ease. His voice and manner suggested culture; he might have been a movie hero right off the set. Debonair was the word Carla thought of.

He strolled across the workshop,

swinging a gold-tipped cane, and smiling. His blue eyes lingered over Carla, admiring the perfection of her figure.

'May I introduce myself?' he said politely. 'Rufus Waldemar, representing the Traders' Insurance Inc. Mr. Mazzini has just transferred to our list.'

Carla didn't say anything. She was looking at Rufus Waldemar and trying to make up her mind about him. The man with the dull eyes and slow-thinking brain didn't say anything either. He waited for orders. Nick snarled savagely.

'You think you can cut in on our racket? You tailor's dummy! I'll carve you into little pieces!'

Rufus Waldemar smiled gently. Not a blond hair fell out of place. He was calm. unruffled, as if he were dealing with a naughty child. He swung his gold-tipped cane jauntily, pushing wood shavings along the floor.

'I'm sure,' he said pleasantly, 'that you won't wish to give trouble. My presence here is to point out that Mr. Mazzini is now under the protection of Traders' Insurance Inc — and that we are in a position to give protection to our clients. You see my point?'

Nick swore virulently.

'You cheap skate!' he snarled. 'You think you can scare us off? You couldn't scare a three-year-old! Joe's paid us protection money for a couple of years — and he's going on paying. You can't cut in on us and get away with it!'

Rufus Waldemar looked at Nick the way a professional looks at an amateur.

'But we have,' he said quietly, swishing his cane. 'Mr. Mazzini is our client — and I, personally, shall see that his shop and person remains unharmed. I suggest that you leave without making trouble — now.'

Nick jeered: 'Look who's talking!'

Carla said: 'You know we represent King Logan?'

Waldemar smiled pleasantly.

'Of course.'

Nick said: 'King runs the protection racket in the Bowery. He's boss of the East Side. You'd better take yourself off to another quarter before King puts the finger on yuh.'

Rufus Waldemar's gold-tipped cane

swished the air and he smiled again. His blue eyes were calm, his slender hands steady.

'King Logan *did* run the protection racket,' he replied gently, 'but he doesn't now. Logan is finished in the Bowery. Traders' Insurance Inc, have taken over for Logan — and Mr. Shapirro, our boss, wishes me to leave this message with you for him. 'King Logan will take himself out of New York if he values his health'!'

Carla said: 'King isn't going to like that. He likes to think he's the boss around these parts. This means trouble.'

Nick said: 'Shapirro is a — !'

The words he used to describe Shapirro left no doubt in anyone's mind that he considered Shapirro to be several times fouler than a ten-year-old cesspool.

Waldemar's eyes hardened and the smile froze on his lips.

'You will,' he said, 'apologise for that.'

Nick snarled: 'Yeah?' and drew a knife. He hurled himself forward at Waldemar.

Carla saw Waldemar's expression change. He no longer looked young. His face was the face of a killer, cold, ruthless. The gold-tipped cane swished up, pointing straight at Nick's chest. Too late, Nick saw the gleaming steel blade shoot out of the cane. He couldn't avoid it because his momentum carried him forward. He groaned as the steel sliced into his chest, slid between his ribs and found his heart.

Rufus Waldemar took a step back, lowering his swordstick. Nick's body slid off the steel and huddled motionless on the floor. Nick was never again going to think he was smart — he was never going to think anything again. He was dead as last year's fashions.

Blood seeped through the beige shirt and spoilt the royal blue tie. The fawn jacket started to discolour, a dark red stain spreading across it. Waldemar wiped the six-inch blade clean and sheathed it. The swordstick became an innocent gold-tipped cane again.

Carla didn't move. She had a gun in her black leather handbag but she didn't bring it out. Her eyes were watching the open door behind Rufus Waldemar and she saw the three hatchet men standing there. Each of them held a heavy automatic, pointing into the workshop.

'A customer for you already, Mr. Mazzini,' Waldemar said. His smile had returned now. He was, once more, the debonair man of the world. He swung his cane jauntily as if he hadn't a thing to bother him.

'King isn't going to like this,' Carla said. 'He's going to come a-gunning for someone.'

Joe Mazzini looked at the ground and scuffed wood-shavings with his foot. His twitch had become suddenly worse.

'You'd better box him, Joe,' Carla said, nodding at Nick.

The heavy man with the flattened nose and dull eyes rubbed one of his scars.

'You want I should take him?' he growled, staring at Rufus Waldemar.

Carla shook her head. 'No,' she said shortly. Ham was a dumb ox; he hadn't noticed the three hatchet men waiting for him to start something. She said: 'Go out to the car, Ham. Wait for me.'

Ham shuffled off. Carla looked at Waldemar, and said:

'Lucky this is a coffin shop. No trouble

about losing a stiff here.'

Rufus Waldemar smiled and bowed.

'You'll convey my message to King Logan?'

Carla nodded. She had a new respect for Waldemar after seeing the cool way he had disposed of Nick. She thought he might give King a little trouble.

'I'll give him all the details,' she said, turning for the door. She paused, and added: 'But he isn't going to like it.'

'That needn't worry you,' Rufus Waldemar suggested. 'I'm sure that Mr. Shapirro would be delighted to welcome such a beautiful girl into his organization.'

'I'll think about it,' Carla drawled. She looked at Joe Mazzini, and said:

'This means trouble, Joe.'

She went through the door, out to the car.

2

Carla's hand gripped the wheel of the car and her foot kept the accelerator hard down. She thought King would want to know what had happened at Joe Mazzini's coffin shop and she was in a hurry. Ham sat beside her not saying anything.

The olive-green Lincoln flashed through the drab streets of Manhattan's Bowery and crossed the East River by Brooklyn Bridge. The night sky was dotted by a million lights from the unshaded windows of New York's skyscrapers. Below, the water gleamed and flowed, and a tug hooted. The skyline was majestic; tall, stately buildings rose almost from the water's edge and the riverfront was noisy with traffic. But Carla had no eye for the scene.

She kept the Lincoln to the centre aisle, passing everything on the road. Once on Long Island, Carla left the main road and threaded her way between dingy Brooklyn tenements. It was an area of squalor, where large families lived cooped up in one room, where children played in the streets, and lines of washing hung in the caverns between giant concrete blocks.

King Logan had been born in Brooklyn and, now that he could afford to move to a more select area, he refused to leave. Brooklyn was home to King Logan and he intended staying there, though now, he lived in a hotel and hired the best suite in the place.

It was called the *Royal*, a name that tickled King's fancy. Carla drove the Lincoln into the all-night garage at the rear of the hotel and she and Ham took the elevator to King's floor.

King Logan was standing by the window, looking out over the river, when Carla hurried in. It was a favourite pose of his, standing there looking out across the river to Manhattan Island; he said it gave him ideas. King had a secret longing to be acknowledged the gang boss of all New York — and Manhattan was most of New York.

He turned as he heard Carla and Ham.

He was tall, over six feet, and well proportioned. He looked as if he had been carved out of muscle and prided himself on being as tough as he looked. His hair was dark and close-cropped and his eyes were too much like round beads and too close together for him ever to be called handsome.

He wore a maroon sweatshirt and grey gaberdine slacks. A green silk dressing gown draped his shoulders, and the right side sagged under the weight of the heavy .45 automatic he kept in his pocket. King never went anywhere without his .45. He said it was his best friend.

His feet were covered by handmade slippers but they were hardly visible for the thick rug that carpeted the floor. King spared nothing to impress his visitors that he was a big-shot. The furniture, the hangings, everything about the suite suggested big money. If King had had any taste it could have looked like an emperor's palace — as he hadn't, it resembled an opulent and gaudy nightmare.

His eyes, when they settled on Carla,

seemed to bore right through her white gown, to caress her from head to toes. He moved towards her, swiftly for so large a man, and brought his hands out of the pockets of his dressing gown. The little finger of his right hand had been shot away at the second joint — the result of a gang fight early in his career — and gave him a sinister appearance.

He caught hold of Carla and swung her off her feet, cradling her warm body close to his chest. His lips sealed hers in a long kiss before she could speak, almost bruising her with the force of his passion. He lowered her to the ground and removed the fur wrap.

Carla gasped for breath. King's passion always roused her; the way he wanted her took her breath away. She stepped back, brushing off his hands, and sat down on a long, low divan.

'Trouble,' she said. 'Nick got his tonight.'

King Logan frowned. His eyebrows seemed to meet in one dark line and his face showed the brutality of his way of life. He glanced at Ham, but Ham's scarred face and dull eyes told him nothing. He turned back to Carla.

'Cops?' he said, His voice was harsh, grating like a file on rusty iron.

'Yeah,' said another voice, 'what sort of trouble, Carla? And what happened to Nick?'

Carla looked towards the bar built into the wall. She hadn't noticed that Jerry was in the room, but then King hadn't given her a chance to notice anything.

Jerry leaned against the bar, a cigarette drooping from his thin lips, a tumbler of whisky in his hand. Jerry usually looked that way. He was King's right-hand man; a thin, lanky man with a mean face. Viciousness gleamed in his eyes and his lean hands were like claws. He never stood upright, but crouched, like a bird of prey about to pounce on its victim.

Jerry wore an exaggerated drape suit with thickly padded shoulders; his shoes were black and shiny and pointed. He looked as if he tapered from wide shoulders to lithe hips to pointed toes. His head was small and seemed incongruous perched atop such exaggerated shoulders.

17

The jacket of his drape was open, hanging free to show the .22 target pistol in the holster under his arm. Jerry was a crack shot with a .22 and didn't need a heavier gun.

Carla wasn't in a hurry to tell her story. King hadn't been very nice to her lately, and now she had the floor, she was going to make the most of it. Carla liked it when she was the main attraction.

'No,' she said softly, 'not the cops. Another gang.'

She relaxed on the divan, leaning back into the cushions, drawing up her dress and crossing her legs. She had nice legs slender and curved and clad in sheer silk hose, and she showed them off whenever she could. No one took any notice.

'What gang?' King Logan demanded harshly.

Carla selected a cigarette, fitted it into a long, jade holder. She placed the holder in her mouth, lit the cigarette, and blew a stream of smoke, very gently, very slowly. *She* wasn't in any hurry — not now she had them waiting on her.

She opened her handbag and drew out

a wad of greenbacks.

'The weekly haul,' she said. 'Five hundred each from Jamie, Franks, Willet, and — '

'Never mind that,' King snapped. 'Tell me about Nick.'

Carla told him. She told him how they'd gone into the coffin shop on Nugget Street how Joe Mazzini had refused to pay any more insurance, how Rufus Waldemar had appeared and Nick had died on the end of his swordstick, how the three hatchet men had stopped her taking immediate reprisals and how Shapirro had warned King to leave town. She *didn't* tell him that Waldemar had suggested she leave Logan and join Shapirro — that was something Carla kept to herself. She thought it might not be a bad idea, if King looked like coming out the loser.

King paced the room, scowling. His voice was bitter and his hands tightly clenched.

'*Me* get out of New York,' he raged. '*Me!*'

He brought out his automatic and

balanced it in his hand.

'If I had Shapirro here — ' His voice died away, but the tone he used left no doubt in Carla's mind that it would have been strictly unhealthy for Shapirro to have shown himself at that particular moment.

Carla smoked her cigarette in silence. Ham wasn't saying anything either. Jerry emptied his glass and lounged across the room.

'What yer gonna do, boss?' he asked.

King roared like a wounded lion.

'Do? I'm not letting any slick shyster like Shapirro run me outa town! I'll blast him and his gang into tiny shreds! I'll — '

'Shapirro's smart,' Jerry said, shaking his head. 'He isn't gonna be easy to get at.'

King calmed down. He pocketed his .45 and walked over to the bar. He poured himself a rye and seated himself next to Carla, on the divan. Absently he stroked her arm while he drank, thinking hard.

Carla was curious about Shapirro. She'd heard of him, but didn't know

enough to gauge the menace he repre-
sented.

'Who is Shapirro?' she asked. 'What's
his angle?'

King said: 'Shapirro's a high-class
racketeer. He operates on West Side;
gambling saloons, dope, women. Anything the suckers in dress suits will pay
for — and they pay big. There's nothing
small-time about Sylvester Shapirro.'

Jerry said: 'Shapirro ain't nice people.
He's a fancy man.' He spat out the words
to show his contempt.

'And now he's horning in on my
territory,' King said indignantly. 'Why
can't he stay on West Side? I don't
interfere with him — why should he try to
cut in on me?'

No one answered that question.

King said, grimly: 'I ain't running from
no fancy guy. If he wants to fight it out,
I'll be around.'

Jerry lit a fresh cigarette. Through the
haze of blue smoke, he observed:

'Shapirro's place is the other end of
Long Island up by Montauk Point. He
never comes out — lives behind a high

wall, guarded by a private army. He's gonna be tough to crack.'

King sipped his rye.

'Yeah,' he said, 'that's right. But his mobsters have got to operate in the open. We'll shoot 'em up. We crack down on every guy who pays Shapirro protection money. And if Shapirro doesn't call it off then, we'll take the boys up to Montauk Point and start a war. We'll blast him out with tommy-guns and pineapples!'

He turned to Carla, and said:

'This Waldemar guy, describe him for me.'

Carla described the debonair man with the blue eyes and gold-tipped cane in detail. King shook his head.

'I've never heard of a guy like that,' he said. 'Have you, Jerry?'

'Naw,' said Jerry. 'Sounds like one of Shapirro's fancy boys to me.'

'You heard of him, Ham?' King asked.

Ham shook his head; his dull eyes registered nothing. Ham wasn't a guy to waste words when a shake of the head would do.

'I guess he must come from outa town,'

King said thoughtfully. 'When I've finished with him, he'll wished he'd stayed there!'

No one mentioned Nick. He didn't count any more. King looked at Jerry and Ham; he said:

'You two beat it. Round up the boys — tomorrow, we start gunning for Shapirro's mob.'

Jerry lounged across the room and went out. Ham lumbered after him. When the door had closed behind them, King looked at Carla.

'Jeez,' he said, 'but you're lovely.'

He hauled her closer and started to kiss her. King was big and strong and she liked the touch of his rough hands on her smooth skin, liked the savageness of his kisses. She clung to him, kissing him back.

* * *

The morning was bright and sunny. Carla drove north, out of New York City, taking the main highway and passing everything on the road. She wasn't in a hurry — she

23

just liked to drive that way. Anything for a thrill. Danger was something she craved.

The sun was bright on the trees lining the road, and on the distant hills, and there was a crispness in the air. But Carla didn't notice. She had other things on her mind. Like the coming battle between King Logan and Shapirro. And thinking about that, brought back the past.

It was nine months since she'd met King and decided he could give her what she craved out of life. Excitement. Carla had always craved excitement — it was in her blood. Blood that went back to the pioneers of the Old West, men who had fought halfway across a continent to make new homes for their families. Carla had been born in the deep south — her mother had died bringing her into the world — and she'd lived there with her father until she was ten. Then Matthew Bowman had moved north to New York.

Old Matthew Bowman was rich by then; his lands brought him millions from white cotton. He bought a large house on Mount Vernon with the intention of giving his daughter, Carla, the finest education money could buy. He wanted her to mix with high society, to learn to conduct herself like a lady of high birth.

But Carla had wild blood in her. At seventeen, she rebelled, walked out of finishing school and got mixed up with a fast-living set of city parasites. She gambled away a small fortune, drank more than she could hold. She was in and out of police courts on charges of dangerous driving, assaulting policemen, and generally misbehaving to the public nuisance.

She lived in nightclubs and gambling dens until her father took to his bed with a heart disease. The doctor said it had been brought on by worrying over Carla. That stopped her cold. Her father was the only person Carla had any feeling for — she reformed, for a time. Then broke out again.

Matthew Bowman, confined to his bed, knew nothing of his daughter's current activities. If he had, he'd have died of shock. Carla was determined he should never learn of her association with King Logan.

She had been just nineteen when she met King. Tired of society life, Carla had gone slumming in the Battery, looking for life in the raw. She'd been attracted to King, thrilled when she learnt he was a gangster with several killings behind him. This, she thought, was the real thing. Life in all its rawness, exciting, dangerous.

She had become King's current flame and joined the gang, collecting protection money, learning to use a gun, to hate the law, to live adventurously. King thrilled her, too. She wasn't in love with him — she'd never loved any man — but she liked it when he took her in his arms. It roused her blood, made her conscious of her beauty, her hold over him. King Logan was tough, a giant of a man, well-muscled, and it gave Clara a sense of power to know that she could control him whenever she wanted.

The car inoved swiftly along the broad avenue, carrying her towards Mount Vernon and her father's home. She visited him once a week, telling lies to account for her absence. Old Matthew Bowman would never learn from her how his daughter was living.

She drove a high-powered, low-slung Chev, not the armoured Lincoln King kept for the gang's use. It climbed the hill towards the rambling old house where her father lay dying. The doctor said he would last a good many years yet — if he didn't have any sudden shocks.

She stopped the Chev outside the steps leading up to the house, jumped out, and went inside. She was wearing a plain skirt of dark brown that hung below her knees, a white silk blouse that showed off her full figure, and a tweed jacket.

She snapped a greeting to the butler and went upstairs. Old Matthew Bowman was sitting up in bed, his face a wrinkled parchment the colour of faded straw. His eyes were faded too, and grey wisps of hair sprouted from his nearly bald head. His forehead was high and broad, all there was left to denote the proud manner in which he had once carried his lean frame. His gnarled hands shook as he held his daughter.

'Hi, Pop,' Clara said brightly, kissing

him with genuine affection. 'How're you feeling today?'

'I'd feel a lot better if you were living here, where I can keep an eye on you,' Matthew Bowman grumbled.

'You don't have to worry about me, Pop,' Carla said quickly. 'I haven't made newspaper headlines since I turned over a new leaf.'

'I guess that's right,' her father sighed. 'A lively young girl like you doesn't want to be tied down. I don't mind you gadding about — so long as you keep out of trouble.'

Carla fussed around, making him comfortable. She had lunch in his room and talked about the good time she was having with a purely fictitious society family. It was a good story and brought a twinkle to Old Matthew's dim eyes.

Around four o'clock, Carla kissed him goodbye.

'Promised to meet someone this evening,' she said. 'See you next week, Pop.'

She went downstairs, out to the Chev, and drove back to Brooklyn and King

Logan. If King was gunning for Shapir-ro's mob, she didn't want to miss any of the fun. And her father need never know . . .

After Carla had left him, Matthew Bowman sat up. His gnarled hand pressed a bell-push and a man came into the room. The man wasn't handsome and his clothes were greasy. He licked his lips all the time. His face was shiny, his manner sly, and his eyes never focused long in one place.

'Well,' demanded Matthew Bowman, 'did you see her, Piggot?'

Piggot nodded.

'Nice-looking girl,' he said, and waited.

Bowman looked steadily at Piggot.

'Carla isn't to know I've set you to watch her,' he said in a strained voice. 'She's got hot blood in her veins and she'd flare up right away if she ever learnt that her father had put a private detective on her heels. But I must know what she's up to.'

He brooded a while before continuing:

'Carla's been *too* quiet lately. It isn't like her at all — I'm afraid she may have got herself into serious trouble and doesn't want to worry me with it. I want you to watch her, see where she goes, who she meets. Don't take any action yourself — report back to me. I'll decide what to do.'

Matthew Bowman smiled a little.

'Carla's growing up. She's a pretty girl — and I don't want her making a bad match. But she mustn't know I'm having her watched — you understand that? Carla's got the real Bowman temper — she'd flare up like a Fourth of July rocket. You're a detective — though you don't look like one! — it's up to you to tail her without being found out. That's all.'

Piggot licked his lips.

'I'll keep on her tail, Mr. Bowman — that's an old job for me. I'll find out what you want and report straight back.'

Old Matthew Bowman lay back on the pillows and closed his eyes. He didn't say any more so Piggot walked out of the room. He went down the stairs and out of the house.

A cinch, this job, he thought; just keep

an eye on some dizzy dame. His face wore a greasy smile as he got in his car and drove after Carla, along the main highway to New York.

Maybe, if he played his cards right, there would be more money to be made out of Carla than her father. If she had a secret and wanted it kept quiet . . . well Piggot wasn't the man to turn down an offer. If it was big enough. He licked his lips as he thought about that.

3

Night was a dark shroud over Manhattan's Bowery. The olive-green Lincoln slid smoothly between gaunt, concrete blocks, gliding with dimmed lights through the rain-washed streets. A fine mist of rain obscured the view for more than fifteen yards and the street corners lacked the usual loungers with wide-brimmed hats and padded shoulders.

Jerry was driving, a cigarette drooping from his thin lips. Ham sat beside him, silent, nursing a sub-machinegun. In the back, King Logan sat with Carla. Carla was dressed in a black velvet gown with bare shoulders and her jet-black eyes were alive with excitement. She gripped her handbag tightly, aware of the revolver it contained.

King's face was impassive. He leaned back, waiting for the Lincoln to arrive at their destination. Behind the Lincoln, two cars followed with King's mob, armed and ready for action. If Shapirro's gang wanted to shoot it out. King wouldn't disappoint them.

Jerry said: 'Coming up to Luigi's, boss.'

King grunted. He took out his automatic, inspected it, slipped it back in his pocket. The Lincoln slowed down and stopped outside a café. Yellow light filtered through the windows and closed door. Inside, Luigi had few customers — business wasn't good on account of the rain

King waited for the first of his two cars to pass him and park a hundred yards further on. He got out of the Lincoln and looked both ways. He watched all the shadows, the dark corners and alleys — and saw no one. He glanced back at his second car, saw that it was parked a hundred yards to the rear. He was covered.

'Keep the engine running,' he grunted to Jerry, and crossed the street.

Carla watched him push open the door of the café and go in. King didn't close the door behind him. He stood a moment, his eyes moving round the tables, stabbing into the doorway behind the counter. Satisfied that none of Shapirro's mob were waiting for him, he went up to the counter.

'Hi, Luigi,' he said.

Luigi grinned weakly. He had a dingy apron tied round his fat belly and a look of apprehension on his round face.

'Good evenin' Mister Logan,' he said eagerly. 'You want Luigi should fix you a hot meal, yes? First class. No charge to you, Mister Logan. On the house, yes?'

King smiled and let his hands rest casually on top of the counter.

'Not tonight Luigi. Just dropped in for a chat. Heard you were paying insurance to a new outfit and wanted to get it straight. For the records.'

Luigi hissed in air.

'No trouble, please Mister Logan. I pay you insurance, two, three years now.'

'Yeah, that's right Luigi, you did. I ain't gonna make trouble — I just wanta get it straight, that's all. You paying another mob?'

The café owner's round eyes looked round his shop. There were a couple of guys talking horses at one table; a girl powdering her face at another. He relaxed a little; King wouldn't start anything with witnesses around.

'Thassa right, Mister Logan,' he said eagerly. 'I pay another firm — Traders' Insurance Inc. They say I pay them or they make big trouble.'

King looked at Luigi thoughtfully. He said:

'I hope they can give you protection.'

He turned and walked out of the café, leaving the door open. He glanced both ways; the street was still deserted. He crossed to the car and opened the door.

'Well?' said Jerry.

'Yeah — Shapirro's cutting in on us,' King said.

He picked up a handgrenade and pulled out the pin.

'But not for long,' he said, tossing the grenade through the open door of the café.

King dived into the Lincoln and Jerry stamped on the accelerator. Carla looked back. She saw yellow light streaming out through the open door. The seconds dragged by, then —

There was a loud explosion as the grenade detonated. A blinding streak of orange flame and clouds of black smoke and dust. A shattering of glass and splintering of woodwork. Twisted steel-work hurled through the air.

King said: 'Luigi ain't gonna pay Shapirro no more insurance — and the other suckers are gonna get the idea he can't come through with any real protection. That's the way I like it.'

King's other two cars were close behind the Lincoln now. Luigi's café was ablaze; angry red tongues of flame shot up into the night air. No one was going to come out of the café to tell the story. When the cops got there. They'd find only charred corpses ... but the other paying clients on King's list would know what had happened.

Jerry chain-lit another cigarette.

'Where to?' he asked.

'We'll call on Toni next — I wouldn't want him to get the idea we don't mean business.'

Jerry turned the Lincoln down side

streets, heading for Toni's shop. King, in the back, hauled Carla closer and started kissing her. He liked to while away the time between jobs — and Carla was always ready for a little love-play.

'Baby,' he said, 'I'm gonna let you take a hand with Toni. This is what you're gonna do . . . '

★   ★   ★

William Franks was no longer a young man. He hitched his drab raincoat tighter about his withered frame as he walked along the dim streets of Bowery. The fine mist of rain had an icy edge to it and Frank was glad he was nearly home, Martha would be waiting with hot muffins and that made him glad he didn't have far to go.

He turned down a dark alley, moving slowly over the cobblestones, feeling for the rickety wooden fence with a shaky hand. He avoided the refuse bins automatically although he couldn't see well in the gloom, he knew every inch of the alley leading to his small house. He'd used the alley every day and night for the past thirty years.

He wasn't very happy about his shop. King Logan took five hundred bucks a week off him for protection — and now that this new firm, Traders' Insurance Inc., was moving in, Franks smelled trouble in the air. Maybe he'd scll up; then he and Martha would be able to retire as they'd always wanted to.

It would be nice to go away with Martha, to forget about Logan and his insurance to leave the Bowery for . . .

'Hullo Franks,' said a quiet voice from the darkness.

Franks peered into the gloom. He made out the form of a blond-haired man in a perfectly cut gaberdine raincoat. He recognized the debonair Rufus Waldemar with his gold-tipped cane.

Two more men moved up out of the darkness and took Franks' arms. They were both lean and muscular with gaunt hatchet faces and cold eyes. Frank began to shake with fear.

'I wondered if you'd thought over my proposition,' Waldemar drawled easily.

'I'm sure you wouldn't want to pass up the chance of taking out insurance with the firm I represent.'

'I can't afford it, Mr. Waldemar,' Franks quavered. 'You know I have to pay Logan and my shop — '

He stopped, gave a cry of pain as one of the hatchet men twisted his arm.

'Logan isn't around to give you protection,' Waldemar pointed out. 'I suggest you come in with us — we can give you the protection you need.'

Franks began to sweat. His old bones creaked as the hatchet man went on twisting his arm.

'I can't pay,' he gasped. 'I don't have the money.'

Rufus Waldemar toyed with his cane. He was still smiling when he drawled:

'That's too bad. You see, I'm afraid we shall have to make an example of you, Franks. I must impress upon Logan's clients his inability to offer them security.' His tone changed abruptly, and he snapped: 'Let him have it!'

Franks tried to draw back. His voice quavered.

'No! Don't — '

The first hatchet man pushed him viciously. Franks stumbled off-balance; his knees banged against a refuse bin and he staggered, his hands clawing at the fence for support. He was too old to put up a fight; too weak, even, to run.

The second hatchet man brought out an open razor. The steel blade gleamed in the dusk as he moved closer. Franks felt his throat constrict.

'No, no!' he croaked. 'Not that . . . arrgh!'

The razor slashed down. The keen blade sliced into his cheek, laying it open. Blood poured out, running down over his collar.

The second hatchet man also had a razor. He slashed Franks across the other cheek. Franks started to scream. His withered arms flailed uselessly as the steel blades came down, again and again.

'Make a good job of him,' Rufus Waldemar said coldly. 'I want these Bowery guys to know we aren't kidding.'

Neither of the hatchet men said anything. They closed in on Franks, going to work with sadistic pleasure. Their arms rose and fell tirelessly; and the razors sliced Franks' face to ribbons.

Franks felt his strength failing. His mouth was full of blood, choking him. His knees buckled and his old frame sagged forward. His hands fell limply to his side — he was too weak even to try to protect himself. The two hatchet men went on carving his face with their open razors; slicing and gouging, slashing and hacking the flesh from the bones.

Franks slumped forward, sobbing. He could no longer see through the red mist before his dimming eyes; the roaring in his eardrums blocked out all other sounds. The agony stabbing his face swept over him in recurring waves, slowly taking away all feeling, all consciousness. He crumpled in a heap on the ground, motionless.

Rufus Waldemar turned the limp body over with the tip of his shoe. He bent over and peered down.

'I think,' he murmured gently, 'that no plastic surgery will ever be able to help Mr. Franks!'

He turned away, followed by the two hatchet men. The car that waited was a large black Rolls. Waldemar and the other two got in. As the Rolls glided away, a door opened and a woman's voice called:

'William? Is that you?'

Rufus Waldemar smiled to himself. He didn't bother to look back. He spoke to the driver.

'We'll call on Toni next. He has a shop in Cork Street. Drive there right away.'

The black Rolls purred through the night and the rain, heading for Toni's shop . . .

Back in the alley, Martha Franks saw the silent body on the ground. She ran forward, crying:

'William . . . William!'

She reached her husband and shrieked with horror. She dropped to her knees, her skirt falling in the mud, the rain washing her face. She cradled her husband in her arms, salty tears staining her wrinkled cheeks. She began to whine in a high-pitched key.

Her eyes stared with glassy despair at the shattered face she had known so well.

Blood seeped over her hands and clothes and the corpse grew cold and stiff under her frail hands.

At last, she stood up. Her grey hair glistened under the raindrops and her face was white and lined with pain. Her thin body shook with anger at the brutality of the unknown murderers. Her tiny hands clenched.

She raised her head to the dull sky and spoke to the cold night air.

'Oh God, give me the strength to bring his killers to justice!'

She turned away, fighting back the tears that threatened to overflow her ageing eyes. She stiffened her frail body with a sudden fixed resolve. Every cent she possessed should go to apprehending the murderers; she would never rest until she had made them pay in full for her husband's brutal death . . . never!

★ ★ ★

The olive-green Lincoln stopped on Cork Street and pulled into the curb. King waited till his other two cars had taken up a covering position, then he turned to Carla.

'That's Toni's shop,' he said, pointing across the street. 'Get him across to the deserted lot behind the wharf — we'll be waiting.'

Carla covered her bare shoulders with a dark cape and clutched her handbag. She slid out of the car and crossed the street. Her eyes were bright with excitement; her dark face flushed. This was living, she told herself. King was going to put Toni on the spot — and she was going to help.

She sauntered past the shop front. A faint light showed through the glass and she saw Toni behind his desk, sorting papers. A thin, youngish man with high cheekbones and a swarthy complexion. A Latin.

Carla put on her act. She was a gay rich girl who'd had too much liquor. She swayed as she walked and started to sing off-key. Toni looked up; his eyes fixed on the lovely girl outside his shop.

Carla was aware she had his attention. She swayed up to a lamppost and clung to it. Clumsily, she started to adjust a suspender.

Toni came out of the shop. Carla heard the doorbell tinkle. She turned, and from the look in his eyes, knew she had him hooked. She dropped her dress and backed away.

'Let me fix that,' Toni said, hurrying after her. 'Come into the shop and we'll fix it good.'

Carla giggled and swayed away, moving down the alley towards the riverfront. Toni went after her. He was young and hot blooded — and here was a beautiful young girl too drunk to know what she was doing. Toni liked 'em that way.

Carla stopped her slurred singing, and shouted:

'*You* can't catch me — I bet you can't catch me, handsome!'

She started to run, weaving an unsteady course across the deserted lot, with Toni in pursuit. The river was a gent murmur of moving water close at hand. The wharves were deserted. It was still and quiet with no sign of King. Only Carla and Toni.

He caught her up, pushed her against a wall so she couldn't get away. Carla let her cape slide off her shoulders and Toni's pulse leapt as he saw her beautiful figure. He grabbed hold of her and kissed her.

'That's enough, Toni!' grated a harsh voice.

The Latin recognized the voice of King Logan. His arms fell away from Carla and he spun round. King held a heavy .45 automatic in his hand and his round, beady eyes were cold as ice.

Just behind King loomed the burly figure of Ham. The scarred face was impassive, the dull eyes emotionless, but he wore brass knuckle-dusters on each hand. Toni didn't like the look of the set-up.

King said: 'You shouldn't chase girls, Toni, it's liable to get you into trouble — especially when she's my girl.'

Toni said: 'Honest, King, I didn't know — '

He broke off, sobbing, as King lashed his mouth with the barrel of his gun. Toni shrank back, spitting blood and holding his face.

'I didn't know — ' he whined.

King snarled: 'You paying insurance to Shapirro?'

Toni said: 'He threatened me, King. Honest, I had to — '

King hit him again with the gun, smashing his jawbone. Toni began to make strange, injured noises. He kept his eyes fixed on King's face as he tried to move away.

King said: 'Beat him up, Ham. I want to make it clear to everyone that Shapirro can't protect his clients.'

Ham moved in, swinging his large fists. He sunk his right into the pit of Toni's stomach; slammed his left into his face. The brass knuckleduster came away covered with blood and skin. Toni whimpered, gasping with pain, trying to move away. Ham kept after him, hitting him.

King stood back, watching. Carla said, over and over:

'Hit him, Ham! Beat him up!'

She was enjoying herself. This was the real thing; more exciting than society life. She felt exhilarated. She liked the way the blood ran down Toni's swarthy face; the animal, sobbing sounds he made as Ham hit him.

Toni couldn't get away. Ham had him cornered and hammered him to a pulp. His right fist crashed into the Latin's nose, breaking the bone at the bridge. Toni covered his face with his hands and Ham kneed him, knocking the wind out of him. Toni doubled up and Ham smashed a cheekbone.

The splintered bone dug into Toni's flesh, making him scream with pain. He fought back, flinging out his arms, trying to keep Ham away. Ham wasn't easily kept away. His arms moved like pistons, in-out, in-out. Toni's eyes puffed up and he staggered blindly, no longer able to see clearly. He walked into Ham's swinging fists and stumbled. Ham hit him across the back of the neck and he slumped forward. Ham kicked his feet from under him.

Carla couldn't keep still. She had a lust for blood. She wanted to hear Toni scream again. She danced round them, shouting:

'Kick him, Ham! Kick him to pieces!'

Ham did his best to oblige. His heavy boots slammed into Toni's body. Toni retched, and he rolled over. Ham booted him in the small of the back, making him stiff with sudden agony. Ham knocked him flat again and kicked him viciously. Toni went slack. He lay in a limp heap, not moving as Ham went on kicking him.

At last, King pulled him off. He said:

'That's enough. *He* won't pay any more protection money to Shapirro.'

Carla said: 'I liked that! Let's beat up some other guy!'

Ham pulled off the knuckle-dusters and wiped the blood. He said:

'You want I should drop him in the river?'

King shook his head.

'Naw. I want him found. When the word gets around the suckers will think twice before paying someone else insurance.'

Ham started back across the deserted lot, towards the car. Suddenly, he stopped.

'Jeez!' he said, pointing. 'I guess — '

He didn't say any more. A fusilade of shots boomed out and a rain of lead swept the open ground. Ham staggered in his stride, nearly chopped in half by tommy-gun fire.

King cursed, and pulled Carla under cover.

'Shapirro's mob,' he hissed, and fired back.

A car lurched across the uneven ground. It was the Lincoln with Jerry behind the wheel. Lead slugs ricocheted off the armoured plates as it careered towards them. In the distance, there was a loud explosion, a puff of orange-red flame and clouds of black, oily smoke. Machine-gun fire chattered angrily. A grenade exploded, blotting out the noise of gunfire.

Jerry flung open the door of the car and King dived into it. The Lincoln was still on the move as King pulled Carla in after him. Jerry drove along the waterfront, skidding round corners, keeping his foot hard down on the accelerator.

King looked back. There were two cars behind now — but they weren't his own boys. The two black Rolls clung to the Lincoln's tail. Someone behind was firing at the tyres. King slid the bullet-proof glass down an inch and shoved the nose of his automatic through the slot. He emptied the magazine at the first of the pursuing cars and hit the front offside wheel. The tyre exploded and the car skidded into a wooden hut, blocking the path of the second Rolls.

Jerry swung the Lincoln down side streets, shaking off pursuit. He eased up a little when it was clear they no longer had anything to fear.

King's face was a livid mask of anger. Carla eased away from him; she'd never seen him like this before.

'What happened back there?' he demanded, his voice shaking with fury.

Jerry lit himself a cigarette and dragged on it.

'Shapirro's mob caught us by surprise,' he said. 'They shot up the boys in the rear car before they had a chance. Then it was a pitched battle; but Shapirro's hoods had their tommy-guns firing first. Not one of our mob got away. I escaped because this car's armoured, otherwise I'd have bought it too.'

King Logan began to curse violently.

'Then we're all that's left of the outfit. You, me, and Carla.'

He brooded on it, then spoke to Jerry.

'We can't go back to the *Royal*. Shapirro will be waiting for us — he won't let us rest now. He'll be out for blood — to finish us off.'

'We pulling out of New York?' Jerry asked.

'No! I'm not running from any fancy guy. We'll hide out till I've got another gang together. Then I'll take Shapirro apart. I'll strew him in little pieces right across Long Island!'

Carla didn't say anything. She was thinking that King was up against the wall, finished. That it was only a matter of time. She remembered Rufus Waldemar's offer. It might not be a bad idea to move into Shapirro's apartment. She thought she'd get a lot of fun with him. Anyone who could shoot up King Logan, and get away with it, was the guy she admired. Only, King mustn't suspect anything . . .

Jerry said: 'Where to?'

King said: 'We'll have to ditch the Lincoln — it's a sign-post right to our door. There's a little dive off the Battery where we'll be safe for a time. The *Water Rat*. We'll go on foot.'

They ditched the car and took the subway down to the Battery. The *Water Rat* was tucked away behind dingy dwelling houses near the docks. It lay squeezed between two warehouses, a tiny, almost subterranean place where sailors could get drunk, or take dope, or get a woman. There was more of it below ground than above and the cellars could be hired by anyone needing to lie low for a time. The police left it strictly alone.

Carla didn't like the look of the place and, anyway, she wanted to contact Rufus Waldemar.

She said: 'I'll go up to my father's place at Mount Vernon. You can let me know when you're ready to start again. I'll rejoin you then.'

King shook his head.

'Don't be a dope. Carla. Shapirro knows you're runnin' with me — if he finds you out in the open, it'll be curtains. You'll stay here. It's safer — anyway, baby, I need you around to help pass the time. I get lonely without you Carla.'

He grabbed hold of her and crushed her vibrant form to his chest, his mouth hot and passionate on hers.

'You're staying with me, baby,' King Logan said hoarsely

Carla surrendered to his lovemaking. King still roused her. He excited her the way no other man ever had. She wrapped her arms round his neck returning his kisses.

She began to wonder when she would be able to slip away from the *Water Rat*, to meet Shapirro and change sides. Well, there was no hurry — Shapirro could wait . . .

4

The apartment house was in downtown Manhattan and Eddie Gifford had to climb three flights of rickety wooden stairs to 37a. He rapped on the door and waited.

The old woman who answered was dressed in shabby black and her grey hairs were streaked with white. Her face, too, was pale, deeply lined. There wasn't much of her; just a frail old woman with shaky hands and something hard and ruthless showing in her narrowed eyes.

'Mrs. Franks?' Eddie asked politely.

She nodded. Eddie shoved a pasteboard card into her hand and waited. Martha Franks read what was on the card:

EDDIE GIFFORD
Private Investigator.

She looked him over very carefully. She decided she liked his tanned face, the humorous quirk to his mouth, his curly brown hair and steady eyes. His eyes were brown too. He had a lithe, athletic figure, well-balanced. He looked like a man who would finish whatever he started.

'Come in,' she said, opening the door wider.

Eddie went in. The room was sparsely furnished, cold. There was a bed, a chest-of-drawers and a chair. The floor was clean and there wasn't any dust on the mantelpiece over the fireless grate. Either Mrs. Franks didn't have much money or she didn't like spending it. Eddie wondered which.

'Please sit down, Mr. Gifford,' said Martha Franks.

Eddie sat in the chair; the old woman perched herself on the edge of the bed. They sat watching each other, not speaking. At last, Eddie spoke:

'What did you want to see me about, Mrs. Franks?'

Martha looked at him steadily.

'I want you to track down a killer,' she said calmly.

Eddie gave a slight start, and waited for the next.

'My husband was beaten up — cut to pieces with razors,' Martha said. She twisted her hands together as she spoke, as if she couldn't get the picture of her husband's face out of her mind. 'I want you to take the case — to find who was responsible and bring him to justice.'

Eddie said: 'That's a job for the police.'

Martha said, bitterly: '*They* won't do a thing. They're too scared. I come from the East Side — the cops don't worry about things that happen on East Side.'

'Tell me about it,' Eddie suggested.

She did. She told him how she and her husband had started a small business, tobacco and papers and children's toys, down in the Bowery. That was thirty years ago. They bought their own house. Life wasn't easy, but they managed. Then, recently, there had been some trouble. A gang had started to threaten her husband, making him pay insurance.

Martha had wanted to sell up and get out, but her husband didn't like running away from small-time racketeers. He paid the money and nothing happened for a time. Then he'd begun to get worried again. He wouldn't tell her what was wrong . . . then he'd been killed. Brutally cut about with razors. And the police shrugged it off like it was normal business practice.

'You know who it was collecting the protection money?' Eddie asked.

Martha shook her head.

'He wouldn't talk to me about it. Said I would worry too much.'

'Not much to go on,' Eddie said. 'What do you want me to do?'

Martha Franks got off the bed and paced the floor Her face was hard and bitter.

'I want his killers,' she said. 'I want to make them pay for what they've done. Not just the men who used the razors — the one behind them. The man who sits back and orders murder so that he can live in luxury. I want you to find the evidence to convict him. I want him to burn!'

Eddie looked at Martha Franks. He saw a quiet, elderly woman whose husband had been brutally murdered; a woman who had lost everything she held dear because someone had wanted some easy money. He said:

'I'll take the job.'

Martha smiled, a strangely cold smile.

'I thought you would,' she said. 'I was told you were an honest copper, Mr. Gifford. That's why I wanted you to take the case.'

She looked round the room, and added:

'You don't have to worry about your fee, I've got the money to pay you. I've sold the business and the house — you can have it all if you get the man I want.'

Eddie said: 'We'll talk about a fee later. Maybe it won't be necessary at all. I don't like thugs who go around beating up old men.'

'You can have the money,' Mrs. Franks said. 'That's why I sold up — why I'm living in one room. So that I've got the money to pay for what I want. Revenge!'

Eddie wandered over to the door. 'I'll take a look round the Bowery. When I find out anything, I'll let you know. And don't worry about the money — you'll need that to live on.'

Martha Franks' face was bitter. 'Once I've got William's killer.' she said calmly, 'I have no further desire to live. Goodbye, Mr. Gifford.'

Eddie said: 'Call me Eddie — Ma!'

He went down the stairs and out into the street, a man with a mission. A mission to track down a killer.

★   ★   ★

The cellar under the *Water Rat* was neither large nor elegant. The stone floor was covered by a thin, worn carpet. The walls were bare. King Logan sat at the wooden table, drinking whisky and watching Carla. His face was a ragged stubble and a cigarette smouldered between his lips.

Carla was fed up. She was used to a gay time, drinks, and bright lights. Being cooped up in a damp cellar was not her idea of fun. Life in the raw had become a little too raw for Carla.

Jerry was stretched out on a camp bed. He stared at the ceiling because King didn't like it when he stared at Carla.

Living three in a room was apt to give the third man of the triangle ideas about the woman. King didn't like it when anyone got ideas about Carla so Jerry stared at the ceiling and chain-smoked. He, too, would be glad when they could move out of the *Water Rat*.

Carla pulled on her stockings fixed the suspenders. She wriggled into the black velvet dress and brushed her hair. She wasn't feeling her best because she wasn't looking her best. Her raven-black hair needed brushing, her face needed a new coat of make-up. Above everything else, she wanted a bath.

She slipped into high-heeled shoes, wrapped the cape about her shoulders. She picked up her handbag, feeling the comforting bulge of the revolver it contained.

King said: 'You didn't oughta leave, baby. It's damn dangerous.'

Carla flared up: 'I'm fed up here. We've been stuck in this filthy hole for three days. I want to hit the high-spots again!'

King didn't say anything. He went on watching her, his right hand sprawled loosely across the table top. His missing finger made him look like a sinister ogre brooding over his victim.

'Don't worry,' Carla said, 'I can look after myself. And I may find out one or two things for you. You'd like to know what Shapirro's doing, wouldn't you? I'll be able to pick up some useful information.'

King appeared to consider it.

'Yeah,' he grunted, 'there's something in that. Maybe you can find out a few things.'

Carla smiled in a satisfied way. He wasn't going to be difficult about it.

'I'll be more help to you outside,' she said softly. 'I can bring you the news, tell you when it's safe to leave, find another hideout. Then you can get a gang together and go after Shapirro.'

King held her close, his hands roving over her lovely figure. He kissed her savagely.

'Yeah,' he said, 'that's OK. And when you come back — ' he kissed her again — 'we'll go to town in a big way. You and me — once I've fixed that smooth shyster Shapirro!'

Jerry sat up. He took the cigarette from

his mouth and said:

'*If* she comes back! I don't like it, King . . . '

King swore and released Carla. He swung across the room and hit Jerry across the mouth, knocking him flat on the bed.

'You shut up!' he snarled. 'Carla's coming back. You've nothing to worry about. Carla loves me don't you baby?'

Carla laughed softly.

'That's right, King . . . I love you!'

She handed Jerry a cold look.

'I'll be back, Jerry — I promise you that . . . '

Jerry didn't say any more. Carla went over to the door and unbarred it.

King said: 'Don't get any ideas, baby. If you double-cross me, I'll spoil that beautiful face of yours. I'll come after you and nothing'll stop me getting you. I don't like double-crossers.'

Carla smiled. She said:

'I'll be back.'

And went through the door, out of the cellar. She heard King bar the door behind her. Yes, thought Carla, I'll be back — with Shapirro!

She went along the stone passage and up the stairs. There was no one to see her and she slipped out by a side door. It was evening. The sky was dark and a mist rolled in off the river, hiding her from the sailors going into the *Water Rat* by another entrance. She heard the sound of women's voices welcoming them.

Carla glided swiftly along the river-front, drawing her dark cape tighter about her. She cut down side streets to the subway and took the train to Brooklyn. She wanted to get herself smartened up before she saw Rufus Waldemar and she didn't think anyone would be watching King's old apartment, not after three days. They wouldn't be expecting him back.

She went into the *Royal* by the back entrance and took the service elevator up to King's floor. She let herself in, went quickly through the rooms to ensure no one was there. Then she stripped off her clothes and ran hot water.

She relaxed in hot, soapy suds, enjoying life. It was good to lay back in a bath once more, after the dirt and squalor of the tiny cellar under the *Water Rat*. Carla dried herself and selected clean clothes; dainty net panties and brassiere to match; black silk stockings and high-heels; a white dress that left her shoulders bare and dropped in flattering lines about her waist and hips. She brushed her soft black hair till it gleamed, fashioned her lips in crimson. She checked the revolver and slipped it back into her black leather handbag — then she was ready to see Waldemar. And Shapirro.

King said that Shapirro operated on West Side, and that's where she went. She took the Chev across Manhattan, driving along Broadway, cutting across Seventh Avenue to the riverfront.

A different riverfront from East Side. Here, the avenues were wide and well-lit; skyscrapers lifted to the night sky, a sky bright with lights and colour. The men wore evening suits and flashed well-filled wallets; the women were exotic, glamorous. This was the quarter where millionaires played.

Carla selected the *Paradise Club*, an

exclusive nighterie overlooking the Hudson. It was a chromium and glitter affair with gambling tables, secluded corners, and several bars. A cabaret was in progress and a line of girls danced across the floor in very little clothing. The men liked it.

Carla perched herself at a bar and watched for Waldemar. She had an idea this was the sort of place he'd frequent She was sipping a highball, waiting, when a man approached. Carla ignored him. She was used to men getting ideas about her and she was only interested in Rufus Waldemar at the moment. But this man refused to be ignored. He gripped her arm and said:

'I want to talk to you in private. Let's go outside.'

Carla was amused by his direct approach.

'Beat it!' she laughed. 'Or I'll call a chucker-out!'

The man said: 'I wouldn't do that. Not if you don't want your father to learn about you and King Logan.'

Carla went cold. She put down her glass and looked steadily at the man. He wasn't much to look at and his clothes were shiny. He had an oily face, a sly manner, but it was his eyes that annoyed her most of all. They wouldn't stay focused in one place but went wandering all over the room as he spoke to her.

'My name's Piggot,' he said. 'I'm a private investigator employed by your father. Now do we talk?'

Carla nodded.

'Let's go onto the veranda, by the river,' she suggested.

Piggot followed her through the French windows. The dance band had started a swing number and the discordant noise followed them outside. Carla stopped by the water's edge, in the shadow of a maple tree. There was no one else about and the sound of the dance band would prevent their being overheard.

'Well?' she said. 'What do you want?'

Piggot grinned.

'Shall we say, seventy-five thousand. For a start?'

Carla looked at Piggot, then down into the dark waters. She knew she was being blackmailed.

'The cops would like to know where King Logan's hiding out,' Piggot said smoothly. 'So would Shapirro. You know — and I know! You see, Carla, I've been trailing you for the past few days. Your father was afraid you might get into trouble, that's why he asked me to keep an eye on you. It's my duty to tell him what I know — unless . . . '

He paused.

'Shapirro would pay plenty to learn of Logan's hideout. You cut me in and maybe I won't tell your father everything. Maybe.'

Carla said: 'You know my father's suffering with heart trouble. If you told him about me, the shock would kill him. It would be murder.'

Piggot shrugged.

'In that case,' he said casually, 'you'd better pay me.'

Carla was furious that her father should hire this greasy pig to watch her movements; then she remembered that Old Matthew Bowman would die if Piggot ever reported back. He couldn't be allowed to report back.

68

Carla hadn't been around with King for nothing. She knew how to deal with Piggot. Her hands felt the shape of the revolver in her handbag and she smiled in the darkness. She turned her head; they were alone. The dance band, swinging into a hot number, was making enough noise to cover up the sound of a shot.

'Well,' demanded Piggot. 'How about it? Do you give me the money — or do I go to your father?'

Carla unfastened her bag. Her hand curled round the ivory butt of the .32. She brought it out, gently eased off the safety catch.

'Yes,' she said softly. 'I'll give you what you're asking for — now!'

She rammed the barrel into his chest and jerked the trigger. The gun kicked back in her hand; the explosion was muffled by his clothes and the noise from the dance band.

The red flame didn't show as the lead slug singed Piggot's clothes and tore into his flesh.

He swayed, moaning a little, holding his hands over his chest. He staggered back from Carla, sagging. Carla gave him a push and he went over the side of the veranda into the river. He made a splash as he hit the water but no one took any notice. Piggot didn't make another sound as he sank into the Hudson. His blood discoloured the water slightly but was soon washed away.

Carla slipped her revolver back in her handbag. She stood looking down into the water, smiling. Old Matthew Bowman would never learn anything from him. Carla felt elated, almost drunk. It was the first time she'd killed anyone herself and she was excited about it. She felt —

'You know,' drawled a quiet voice behind her, 'even lovely young girls are not supposed to shoot their admirers at the *Paradise Club*!'

Carla gasped, and turned to face Rufus Waldemar.

5

Waldemar swung his gold-tipped cane with a jaunty air. His handsome face was half in shadow and his blond hair gleamed in the reflected light from the nightclub.

Carla hastily composed herself. She said, easily:

'I was looking for you.'

'Really?' Waldemar seemed politely incredulous. 'Not,' he added, 'to shoot me, I hope?'

Carla said: 'I want to see Shapirro.'

Waldemar smiled and swung his cane.

'An odd coincidence. Mr. Shapirro wants to see *you*. It should be quite a party.'

He sauntered closer and looked over the veranda into the water. But the man who had gone over had drifted downstream and there was nothing visible to mark the spot.

'Tell me,' Waldemar said politely, 'who

was he? An old beau you got tired of? A wolf with persistence? Or did he just have the kind of face you can't stand?'

Carla said: 'His name was Piggot and he was a private detective. He was trying to blackmail me.'

'Ah,' purred the blond man, 'a detective. That accounts for the fact he was watching Logan's apartment — as I was myself. He followed you, and I followed him. Quite amusing really. If it's any satisfaction to you, I am strongly in favour of your shooting every detective you meet, but be careful of blackmailers — some of my best friends indulge in *that* pursuit!'

'Let's get away from here,' Carla said impatiently.

Waldemar laughed softly.

'From the scene of the crime? You know, the police have a theory that a murderer always returns to the scene of his crime. Personally, I *never* do . . . '

He took her handbag, opened it. He removed the revolver and put it in his pocket, then returned the bag.

'I feel safer,' he murmured, 'when the

girl I'm with is unarmed.'

His manner changed abruptly. He caught her in his arms and pressed his mouth firmly on hers.

'Lovely,' he crooned, 'so lovely . . . '

Carla couldn't get away. She found he was remarkably strong for so slender a man. His arms gripped her with bruising force as he kissed her, kissed her long and hard.

Carla relaxed and let her vibrant form press against him.

'Cut that out, Glenn,' another voice said sharply. 'We've no time to waste.'

Carla looked over Waldemar's shoulder. She gave a little cry of surprise when she saw another man, identical in build and face. He, too, had blond hair, a debonair manner, and was dressed in grey. He, too, swung a gold-tipped cane.

The man who had been kissing Carla said:

'You always interfere at the wrong moment, Rufus. And I wasn't wasting time — that would be impossible with any girl so beautiful as Carla!'

Carla looked at them and wondered

which was which.

The newcomer said:

'I'm Rufus — we met in Joe Mazzini's shop, remember?'

Carla nodded. The first man said:

'I'm Glenn Waldemar — we're twin brothers. Confusing, isn't it?'

Rufus said, impatiently: 'The car's waiting. Carla, you're coming with us to see Shapirro.'

They moved into the light and Carla saw that the twins were identical — except for one odd detail. Rufus had blue eyes; Glenn had one blue and one brown eye. It gave an odd, menacing cast to his handsome face.

The Waldemar twins took Carla through the club to the black Rolls that waited by the curb. The driver wore a drape suit and a hard face. Carla sat between the twins as the Rolls moved off.

Glenn offered Carla a cigarette, which she accepted. She lay back in the car, smoking.

'You know, Carla,' he said softly, 'I hope you and I are going to get better acquainted.'

'Don't get an ideas,' Rufus said to his twin brother. 'Shapirro doesn't like his women to be mauled around.'

Carla snapped: 'I'm nobody's woman!'

Neither Rufus nor Glenn replied, but Glenn's face went sullen. The black Rolls skirted Central Park and crossed the East River by the Queensboro' Bridge. On Long Island it headed north, travelling with speed along the broad highway.

The moon came out, flooding the countryside with silvery light, giving the trees a ghostly appearance. Carla sat tight, wondering what Shapirro was going to be like. She'd heard a lot about him, now she was going to learn for herself.

She wasn't afraid. She felt confident she could hold any man's attention with her beauty; knew, too, that he would be interested in King's hideout. He'd be grateful if she told him where to find King and Jerry. Carla smiled contentedly.

She had no doubt that Shapirro would take her into his gang. It was a pity King would have to die, but there'd be compensations — Shapirro would see to that. Or, maybe, Glenn Waldemar. She thought Glenn would be a worthy successor to King.

The Rolls had reached a flat stretch of open country. To the right, an expanse of yellow-brown sand stretched to the sea. Inland, the sand merged into wild scrubland. They were very near the northernmost tip of Long Island, Montauk Point, where Shapirro had his headquarters.

She saw the house in the distance, gleaming palely in the moonlight. It stood on top of a rise, a vast, rambling house surrounded by a high wall. The far side ran to the cliff edge and the Atlantic breakers pounded the rocks below.

The Rolls stopped at the gate. Carla watched steel doors open, saw the guards with tommy-guns, heard the baying of dogs. As the car took her up the drive to Shapirro's house, she had a moment of uneasiness. If things didn't go as she planned, it wasn't going to be easy to get out. It was going to be impossible.

She went into the house, through a wide door, escorted by the twins. They took her through a hallway tiled in black and white. The walls were a flat white, the ceiling dead black. Concealed lighting cast sombre shadows on the wide staircase that spiraled upwards.

The balcony was black and white; exquisite statuettes of black jade perched in alcoves; silver figurines gleamed against velvet backcloths. The lighting did weird things to the black-and-white motif.

The Waldemar twins marched Carla along the balcony and through heavy black curtain. Beyond swinging glass doors was a fabulous room — and Sylvester Shapirro.

★   ★   ★

Eddie Gifford hadn't been wasting time. He interviewed shopkeepers in the Bowery, hunting for a clue to the killer of William Franks. But the people who paid protection money were wary about talking to strangers. Their eyes shifted uneasily; their hands betrayed their nervousness. They didn't want to take a beating the way Toni had; or have their shop blown up with a grenade; or have their faces slashed with razors. They didn't talk.

So Eddie haunted the bars where small-time crooks hung out. A few high denomination dollar bills changed hands and he began to get the story. How King Logan had been boss on the East Side till Shapirro's mob moved in; how Logan's gang had been shot up in a gunfight; and how Logan had disappeared, leaving Shapirro in control of the rackets.

The more Eddie learnt, the less he liked it. He was up against big stuff and he doubted his ability to handle it alone. He couldn't get a lead on King Logan — maybe the gangster had left New York for a safer place. That would have been wise but, somehow, Eddie doubted it. From what he heard about Logan, King wasn't a quitter.

Shapirro was even harder to locate. Eddie picked up tales of the twin blond killers and their hatchet men, but he never got a direct lead on Shapirro. Only rumours. And the rumours weren't pleasant.

He deducted that it was Shapirro's

mob who had killed Martha's husband from the fact that William Franks had been paying Logan; King would, therefore, have no cause to beat him up. But getting evidence against Shapirro was going to be tough.

He talked it over with a lieutenant of police.

'Shapirro?' The lieutenant shrugged. 'We know he's behind the worst rackets in the city. Dope, women, killings — nothing's too bad for Shapirro. But we can't get anything on him. He has a ritzy joint up at Montauk Point and never leaves it — all the dirty work is done by hirelings. And there are plenty of guys down at City Hall ready to cover for him — Shapirro has money. And money talks!'

So Eddie called on the G-men.

'Sure,' they said, 'we know about Shapirro. One day he'll make a slip — then we'll pounce. But we can't move against him till we get proof — he's too powerful. Bring us the evidence and we'll grab him fast!'

Eddie went back to the drab room where Martha eked out her existence and reported. She listened to him in silence.

'Shapirro!' She rolled the word round her tongue and spat it out. 'That's the one I want — the others aren't important. You'll get Shapirro for me, Eddie?'

Eddie Gifford frowned.

'That won't be easy,' he said.

Martha watched his face as he brooded over the problem. 'You've got a plan,' she said softly. 'I can tell by your face.'

Eddie nodded.

'The way I see it is to force Shapirro out into the open. Make him declare his hand. And the man to do that is — King Logan. I want to play one against the other. Maybe I'll get something the G-men can use — it's worth trying anyway.'

'You said Logan had disappeared,' Martha objected.

'I figure he's hiding out someplace, waiting for the chance to strike back. I've got to find him — give him a little help to get at Shapirro.'

Eddie thought for a while, then said: 'Logan was living with a dame called

Carla. He'll want to contact her if she's not with him. I guess she'll be the one to lead me to him.'

'Carla?'

'Yeah,' Eddie said. 'I've been checking up on her. Her full name's Carla Bowman — she's a society dame gone wild. Her old man has a house at Mount Vernon — I think I'll pay him a visit to see if he knows where his daughter is.'

Martha said: 'I don't care how you do it — but get Shapirro for me!'

Eddie nodded silently. He left the apartment and went down to the street. He got in his car and drove north to Mount Vernon and Matthew Bowman.

6

The glass doors swung silently shut behind Carla. The room was large with a high ceiling and, once more, the black-and-white motif dominated. She stood still, forgetting the Waldemar twins at her side, studying the room and its occupant.

The walls were panelled with black glass giving an effect of distance, as if the room receded into a fantasy world of its own. The floor was tiled in black and white; the ceiling was an oppressive blackness. Concealed lighting sprawled sombre shadows over the transparent plastic furniture and a heavy scent of burning incense pervaded the air.

Behind a fantastic desk of clear plastic sat Sylvester Shapirro. He wore a black suit with a white shirt and black bow tie. His face was chalk-white and the lighting, flattering as it was, could neither conceal the lines of dissipation about his mouth nor the pouches under his eyes. Queer eyes, small and pink. His hair was a mass of snowy white growth that made his head appear unnaturally large for his body.

One of the twins said: 'This is Carla — Logan's dame.'

Shapirro looked, at Carla with his small pink eyes and made her feel uncomfortable. He didn't look at her the way other men did. He didn't rise or say anything. Only his hands moved.

On the desk before him lay a thin leather whip and Shapirro's fingers played with the lash. There was something terrifying in the way he stroked the lash, looking at Carla with his pink eyes. Carla began to feel scared.

She fought to control herself, made her hips sway voluptuously as she moved nearer. A faint smile played across Shapirro's lips. His face cracked into a thousand tiny lines.

'You are very young, Carla,' Shapirro said. His voice was an eerie whisper that seemed to go all round the room and come echoing back from the black glass walls.

Carla realized, with a shock, that he was very old. That was something she hadn't expected. Why, he must be over seventy!

Shapirro licked his cracked lips.

His whispering revolted her. The way his pink eyes lingered on her figure was somehow obscene. 'I collect beautiful young girls, Carla . . . I shall be pleased to add you to my collection!'

His eyes moved steadily over her, admiring the contrast of her raven-black hair and dark skin against the white dress. He didn't hurry with his inspection, took his time over her smooth oval face and wide jet-black eyes, her bright crimson lips. He liked the way the filmy material clung to her waist and hips, accentuating the beauty of her curves; he saw the outline of her legs, long and slender and full of youth.

Sylvester Shapirro sighed gently.

'So much beauty — and so fragile!'

Carla shrank back from his gaze. His pink eyes seemed to undress her. She began to wish she were back with King. She flung an appealing glance at Glenn;

the blond man with different coloured eyes desired her. That was something Carla could understand — not this frightening way Shapirro had of staring at her.

Shapirro caught Glenn Waldemar's look.

'You will not look at Carla in that manner, Glenn,' he whispered. 'She is mine — all mine. Be careful, Glenn — you know what will happen if you disobey me.'

Glenn's face went sullen and he looked away. He didn't say anything, but his cane swished the air viciously.

'I came of my own free will,' Carla said, summoning her courage. She felt she had to stand up to Shapirro now if she were to save herself. 'I thought you might be able to fit me into your organization. I can be of use to you — I know where King is hiding out. You want to know that, don't you?'

Shapirro chuckled softly.

'So, you can see the writing on the wall, Carla. You can see that Logan is finished — and want to change sides. You're a smart girl!'

Carla went closer, smiling provocatively. She swayed her body the way she used to do to control King.

'I like excitement. I like danger, and adventure. I got all that with King — maybe I can get more with the man smart enough to put him out of business.'

'Tell me,' whispered Shapirro, 'where can I find King?'

Carla didn't hesitate. She had to win Shapirro's confidence. She said:

'You'll find him in one of the cellars under the *Water Rat*, down in the Battery. He's only got Jerry with him. If you like, I'll guide your men there.'

Sylvester Shapirro smiled coldly.

'That won't be necessary. Rufus and Glenn will go. They are quite capable of finding their way — and I want you here. You interest me, Carla — and this might be a trap set by Logan. If so, you'll regret your part in it. Logan had better be there or — '

'He's there,' Carla said quickly.

Her heart sank. She didn't want to remain alone with Shapirro. She didn't feel safe with him. She wanted to get out

86

of the room with the black-and-white motif, away from this old man who collected young girls. And she had to stay . . .

Rufus and Glenn Waldemar went out through the swinging glass doors and disappeared behind the black drape.

'Take a look behind the curtain,' Shapirro whispered, pointing to an alcove in one of the black glass walls.

Carla crossed the room and drew back the curtain. Her breath hissed in a sudden intake as she stared at an empty black coffin with silver handles. There was a silver nameplate with a name engraved and filled-in with black. The name was:

KING LOGAN

Carla let the curtain fall back. She turned to look into small pink eyes.

'Logan,' came Shapirro's eerie whisper, 'was in my way. I smashed his gang because I wanted control of the East Side. You see, Carla, I want to operate on East Side the way I do on West Side. I want to control all the rackets in New

York. Manhattan, Long Island, New Jersey — they'll all fall to me in time.'

His pale hands played with the whip on his desk as he spoke.

'Taking over the Bowery is only one step in expanding my empire. Logan had to be removed. Now, he must be killed, because a cornered rat is dangerous. Rufus and Glenn will take care of that.'

He stopped talking and just looked at her. Carla wanted to run, but she knew there was no sense in that. The house was too well guarded, the wall too high. And there were the dogs. She had to stay and bluff it out — but once she got away, she'd take good care she never got in Sylvester Shapirro's hands again.

The white-haired man spoke again.

'I've found out quite a lot about you, Carla. Your father, for instance, suffers with a heart disorder — and you take good care he doesn't learn of your somewhat unconventional way of life. Perhaps the shock would be too much for him?'

He lifted the whip and flicked it gently. The lash curved through the air and touched Carla's cheek.

'So,' he said softly, 'you will do whatever I ask — or your father will get a shock that may prove fatal.'

'The last man to threaten me in that way,' Carla snapped, 'is dead!'

Shapirro chuckled.

'But here,' he whispered, 'I give the orders. You will not be able to kill me so easily.'

Carla's eyes blazed. If Glenn Waldemar hadn't taken her revolver, she'd have shot Shapirro dead and taken her chances on getting away. But she was unarmed, a prisoner in this fantastic house.

'If you tell my father anything about me,' she said coldly, 'not all your gunmen will be able to save you. I'll tear you to pieces!'

Shapirro's hand crawled across the desktop and he pressed a button. Somewhere, chimes tinkled melodiously.

'You've got spirit,' he chuckled. 'I want you to see what happens to girls with spirit.'

Carla found herself holding her breath. A door opened and a girl came in. She was tall and blonde, about twenty-two, a good-looking girl with a well-developed figure.

'This is Phyllis,' Shapirro murmured, 'one of the many lovely girls I keep for my delight. Beautiful, isn't she?'

Carla had difficulty in holding her tongue. She wanted to tell Shapirro what she thought of old men who kept girls like this. The blonde was dressed in a black gym tunic that would have fitted a schoolgirl. Her full figure thrust out over the top of the briefs. Her legs were bare and she perched ridiculously on shoes with six-inch heels. She had a black bow in her hair.

Phyllis curtsied to Shapirro.

'You wanted to see me, my lord?' she asked.

Her voice was flat, toneless. Her face lacked all expression. Her eyes were without the vital spark that marks a human being from an animal. Something had happened to her to break her spirit. Carla turned away, revolted.

'Come here, Phyllis,' Sylvester Shapirro said softly.

The blonde went over to him, stood motionless. Shapirro's hand stroked her smooth skin. Phyllis began to quiver, and fear showed in her eyes, but she didn't move away. She stood there and let the old man with white hair stroke her.

Shapirro said: 'That's all, my dear. You can go back to the others now.'

The blonde curtsied again and moved away. Shapirro lifted his whip and flicked it. The lash curved through the air and caressed the blonde's legs, leaving a faint red mark. She took no notice, went out through the door.

Carla's face was white. She felt something choking her. She was disgusted — and afraid — of Sylvester Shapirro and his unnatural desires. She wished she'd stayed with King. At least, he wanted her the way a man should want a woman . . .

'She's doped,' Shapirro said. 'Full of the stuff. It breaks their spirit, makes them more amenable to my little fads.'

Carla said: 'I'll be more use to you the way I am.'

Shapirro smiled.

'Perhaps,' he whispered. 'We must wait

and see what the twins find at the *Water Rat*. Perhaps, if you spoke the truth about Logan's hiding place, it won't be necessary to treat you in that manner. Though you would be an asset to my collection . . . '

'King will be there all right,' Carla said confidently.

'Let us hope so,' Shapirro murmured. 'I keep an establishment especially for breaking-in girls — I doubt if you'd like it there. But that's what will happen to you . . . if Logan isn't dead when the twins report back!'

His pink eye went to the clock on the wall.

'They should be at the *Water Rat* by now,' he whispered. 'Rufus will telephone in a little while.'

Carla tried to forget she had told him where to find King. She tried to forget the way King had held her in his arms and thrilled her. He'd be dead soon — and it was she who would have killed him. She wanted to forget she had exchanged King for Sylvester Shapirro . . .

The old man with white hair and pink

eyes went on looking at her, quietly enjoying her discomfort. He spoke again.

'When I travelled in the East, many years ago now, I learnt of the custom of keeping a harem.' He chuckled. 'It was always my ambition to maintain a selection of young girls — see . . . '

He pressed another button on his desk. Immediately, one of the black glass, walls changed, became transparent. Carla could see into the next room, a large, well-lit room where beautiful girls in scanty costumes reclined on cushions. They posed for Sylvester Shapirro the way they had been trained to do — and not one of them showed a trace of emotion in her face. They were all doped into submission.

Carla felt her blood freeze. She wanted to get away — desperately, she wanted to leave this crazy house where an old man indulged his strange desires. She felt the walls closing in on her. She felt her legs weaken and her mind reel. She seemed to be floating down a spiral staircase . . .

The ringing of a telephone bell brought her back to reality. Shapirro lifted the receiver and acknowledged the call.

'Rufus? Yes . . . I see. Yes, you'd better come back — I've another job for you. Yes, at once!'

Carla watched him lay down the telephone. His pink eyes fixed on her and his lips curved in a smile. A cold, cruel smile.

He whispered: 'Logan was not at the *Water Rat!*'

Carla shrank back.

'He *must* be! I tell you — '

Shapirro rose from his seat. He pressed a button on the desk and chimes sounded again.

'You tried to double-cross me, Carla. You know what to expect.'

'No! King was there — I swear he was! Don't make me like the others — oh, God!'

Two men came silently through the door. Lean men with hatchet faces and cold eyes.

'Hold her still,' Shapirro whispered.

Carla tried to run, to get past them, through the door.

They took her arms, gripped her

tightly. She began to rave, hardly knowing what she was saying. She saw Shapirro coming towards her, his mop of snow-white hair bobbing gently, his pink eyes glittering.

They held her down on the desk, twisting her arms till it was agony to move. One of the hatchet men hit her, knocking all the air out of her. Carla lay still, tears streaming down her face.

She couldn't move an inch. She watched Shapirro take a small case from a drawer in the plastic desk. He opened the case and brought out a hypodermic syringe and a phial of colourless liquid. He filled the syringe and looked along the needle, still smiling.

'This won't hurt you, Carla — just a prick of the needle and it's all over.'

She tried to struggle, but the two men held her rigid. She couldn't get away. She began to scream. One of the hatchet men hit her in the mouth and her screaming changed to a choked sobbing. She watched Shapirro come closer. He dabbed an antiseptic on her arm; brought the needle nearer.

She felt the prick as the needle plunged into her skin — saw the level of the liquid in the syringe go down as the dope was forced into her veins. Her head began to swim.

A veil swept over her eyes. She saw Shapirro's face looming over her — blurring — changing shape — the room receded, faded . . .

She was falling into a bottomless pit. Down a dark tunnel to a whirlpool at the bottom. The whirlpool sucked her under, stifling her, blocking out all light. She was in darkness — all consciousness gone . . .

7

Jerry rubbed his bruised lips and lit a fresh cigarette. He watched King Logan bolt the door after Carla had left. He said:

'I don't like it. I don't trust that dame.'

King snarled: 'Shaddup!'

Jerry dragged on his cigarette, watching King. He couldn't understand the way King felt about Carla. Sure, she was a looker, had a swell form and class, but hell, a guy didn't have to act like she was the only dame in the world. Jerry had made plenty of dames — but he didn't drool over them. When he'd had his fun, he kicked them out — fast.

He said: 'What's eatin' yuh, King? She's double-crossing us, all right — she'll be running to Shapirro and leading him straight here. You gonna wait to be rubbed out?'

King hurled an empty glass at Jerry.

'Carla's OK,' he snapped. 'You shut up about her — she'll be back.'

He slumped in his seat and tossed back a tumbler of whisky. His close-set eyes gleamed in the yellow light and he rubbed an unshaven jaw with his hand; the missing finger made his hand appear like a malformed claw.

'Carla's all right,' he repeated.

Jerry didn't say any more. He looked round the tiny cellar and began to think how much it was like a prison. The thin carpet and bare walls; the single door. If Shapirro's mob found them, they wouldn't have a chance. They'd be like animals in a trap, waiting to be executed.

Suddenly, he couldn't stand it any more. He swung his feet off the bed, onto the ground. He stood up, moved over to the door.

King watched him suspiciously.

'You going someplace, Jerry?' he asked.

'Yeah, I'm getting outa here. You can stay for that crazy dame to bring Shapirro's killers here — not me. I'm getting out while I can still walk.'

'Carla won't double-cross me,' King said. 'Sit down and take it easy. Carla's one dame I trust.'

Jerry said: 'Nuts!'

King watched him unbar the door and fury swept over him. Jerry had kept in line all the while things had been going smoothly; now that they were on the run, he wanted to get out. Desert him. King's lips curled. He no longer had any use for Jerry.

He brought out his .45, pointed it at Jerry's back. Smiling coldly, he squeezed the trigger. The shot boomed deafeningly in the tiny cellar. The heavy slug tore into the small of Jerry's back, the soft nose spreading out. King always used slugs with soft noses because they killed slower and gave more pain.

Jerry writhed on the floor, moaning, a bloody froth bubbling from his thin lips. He twisted sideways, brought out his .22, aimed it at the man who had shot him in the back.

King fired again, sent the .22 target gun sliding across the floor. He went over and kicked Jerry in the guts.

'You cheap, yellow four-flusher,' he snarled. 'No one says my dame is a double-crosser!'

Jerry winced, and began cursing. Then King squeezed the trigger again.

Jerry's head was almost blown off by the shot. His body convulsed once, then lay still. King stood over him, his face dark; Jerry wasn't going to walk out on anyone again.

It was strangely quiet after the echoes had died away; the air was acrid with cordite fumes. King looked down at the corpse, thinking: he couldn't stay at the *Water Rat* now. He had to get away, find another hideout. And get in touch with Carla.

He went through the door and along the cellar. Steps took him up to ground level and he let himself out by a side door. No one saw him leave. Outside, it was dark. The night air was cold on his skin and the river lapped at the jetty a little way off.

King moved swiftly, silently, along the dingy streets of the Battery. He had made up his mind. He was going out to Mount Vernon, to Carla's home. He'd stay there till she showed up. It would be a good hideout — Shapirro wouldn't think to look for him there. And it would make a swell headquarters when he got a new gang together. If Carla's old man started anything, well, it would be just too bad for him . . .

King stole a car and drove north to Mount Vernon. He ditched the car where it would give no clue to his destination and started walking. He didn't mind doing the rest of the journey on foot — not with a safe hideout waiting at the end of it.

He swung along the road, his face brightening as he thought of Carla. She was a swell dame; society too. It would be nice to hold her again, to feel her cool lips against his. Maybe she'd be waiting for him at Mount Vernon . . . he began to hurry.

★ ★ ★

Sunlight streamed its brilliance over the Mount Vernon hills as Eddie Gifford swung his car up the drive leading to Matthew Bowman's home. Eddie decided he liked the house. It was quiet, an old

Colonial mansion, with wide windows and stone terraces. Ramblers clung to the stone face and twined about the pillars.

Eddie went up the steps and thumbed a bell push. The butler was smooth-shaven and plump. Eddie handed him his card and said:

'Is Carla at home?'

The butler stiffened.

'Miss Bowman,' he replied distantly, 'is away.'

Eddie stuck his foot in the door to prevent the butler closing it in his face.

'I'd like to see Mr. Bowman,' he said, smiling.

'Mr. Bowman,' said the butler, stiffly, 'is not well. He does not see visitors.'

Eddie leaned on the door a little, and walked inside.

'Suppose you take him my card and ask if he'll see me,' he suggested. 'Tell him I want to have a talk with his daughter.'

The butler hesitated.

'Miss Carla,' he asked, 'is she in some kind of trouble?'

Eddie shrugged.

'Maybe. I could tell better if I knew

102

where to find her.'

The butler seemed to be struggling with his conscience. At last, he padded softly upstairs, returning shortly.

'Mr. Bowman,' he said, 'will see you. This way.'

Eddie followed him up the stairs and along a passage. The butler paused outside an oak panelled door.

'I hope you'll excuse me mentioning it, sir,' he said apologetically, 'but the master's heart . . . he is in no condition to hear anything unpleasant. The shock would be too much for him.'

Eddie nodded gravely.

'I'll watch it,' he said, and went in.

Matthew Bowman was sitting up in bed waiting for him.

Eddie saw the proud, high forehead, the faded eyes; saw too, the lines of worry etched across the parchment face.

'Carla?' said the old man in a pleading voice. 'She's not in trouble?'

Eddie thought she might be, but he didn't say so.

'Not so far as I know,' he said reassuringly. 'I've never met your daughter, Mr.

Bowman — but I'd like to.'

'Your card,' Old Matthew croaked. 'You're a detective — '

'Private investigator — nothing to do with the police,' Eddie replied. 'A client of mine wishes to trace a man called King Logan. I was told that your daughter might be able to help me locate him, that's all — a routine investigation.'

Matthew Bowman didn't seem as relieved as he should have been. He studied Eddie carefully; his tanned face and steady brown eyes, the humorous quirk to his mouth.

He seemed satisfied with what he saw.

'I've never heard of anyone called Logan — my daughter's never mentioned him.' Old Matthew brooded a while, then added: 'Mr. Gifford, have you ever met a private detective named Piggot?'

Eddie shook his head.

'I hired him to keep an eye on Carla,' Bowman said. 'She's young and a little — er — wild, and I was afraid she was in some kind of trouble. Piggot was supposed to report back to me. He hasn't — and I haven't heard anything from

Carla. I'm worried about it.'

Eddie thought: a tec watching Carla — and he'd disappeared. With Carla running with Logan, and Shiparro cutting in on them, it was only too likely that Piggot had stopped a lead slug. He didn't think Bowman would be hearing from Piggot.

'Do you know where I can find Carla?' he asked. 'Or where Piggot went before he stopped reporting?'

Matthew Bowman shook his head.

'Carla comes and goes as she pleases,' he grumbled. 'I never know where she is. And Piggot never reported at all.'

Eddie sighed. It looked as if all the leads were blind. He was getting nowhere.

'I'd like to hire you to find Carla,' Old Matthew said, struggling with the words. 'Help her if she's in some kind of jam. She's all I've got and I don't want anything to happen to her.'

Eddie looked at Matthew Bowman. He felt sorry for the old man; he didn't look the sort of man who deserved the kind of daughter he had.

'I can't take on two jobs at the same

time,' he replied. 'It isn't ethical — but if I run across Carla, I'll see what I can do. Maybe I can persuade her to return to the fold.'

Bowman sighed with relief.

'I wish you would, Mr. Gifford.'

Eddie shook the old man's hand and left the room. Outside, he went down the stairs and out to his car.

He didn't think it likely he'd be able to do anything with Carla. Not if she were in deep with King Logan. Not if Shapirro was gunning for her. He shook his head sadly: Bowman was due for a shock in the near future and Eddie doubted if he'd get over it. He wouldn't have betted on Matthew Bowman living to a ripe old age.

He drove slowly back to the big city. What now? He still had to find Logan somehow. And Carla, where was she? With King? Or had Shiparro found them first?

Eddie found a bar and did some steady drinking. It didn't help him find Logan or get anything on William Franks' killer, but it did stop him wondering about an old man whose daughter had gone wild. And that was something.

8

First there was a grey mist. She floated slowly to the surface, wondering if it were all a dream. Consciousness came back by degrees. She was aware of a blinding light that filtered through the mist, hurting her eyes. Strange objects floated about and, after a time, settled into the walls of a room. Strange walls that might have been padded with rubber-sponge.

She was in bed, tightly tucked in. Something coarse chafed her skin, irritating her. She moved, slowly because her body didn't seem to respond properly; her arms crawled sluggishly. She struggled into a sitting position, feeling her body with her hands.

Where was she? The pyjamas she wore were made of rough linen; it had been this that irritated her. She tried to get out of bed and found she couldn't — something dragged on her leg. With difficulty, she felt under the clothes, ran her hand down her leg till it touched a metal band fixed round her ankle. A chain ran from the metal band to the end of the bed.

Why was she chained? She tried to think clearly — even had trouble remembering her own name. Then it came back to her. *Carla*.

Her arm hurt. She pulled up the sleeve of the pyjama jacket and rubbed the spot. There was a tiny mark as if a needle had been jabbed in, and this worried her. She couldn't remember —

She must have had an accident, that was it. She was in hospital. But they wouldn't have chained her to the bed. Her eyes fixed on the padded walls again . . . padded! She caught her breath. Surely she couldn't be — *insane*?

It hit her, jolted her out of the grey mist. She became aware that she wasn't alone in the room. There was another bed with another girl — a blonde. This girl was pretty, except for the lack of expression on her face. She had a smooth skin and the sort of figure showgirls have. She too, was chained. She was murmuring, over and over, in a dull monotone:

'I must do as my lord commands. I must do as my lord commands.'

Over and over, without stopping, without varying her tone. It got on Carla's nerves. She snapped:

'Shut up!'

The other girl took no notice. She went on muttering to herself. Carla studied the room more closely. Yes, she was in a padded cell — there could be no doubt about it. The walls and floor were quite bare except for the rubber-sponge. The steel door looked quite immovable and, through the slots in a metal grille, she looked out into a whitewashed corridor.

Her bed was fixed rigidly to the floor and she was chained to the bed. The bright light came from a concealed tube high in the ceiling, far out of reach. She began to panic. How long had she been like this? She wasn't mad — she felt all right now. They had no right to keep her chained up. She calmed herself. The doctor would see she wasn't insane when he came, then she'd be released. She told herself this several times.

The other girl was still muttering:

'I must do as my lord commands . . . I must do as my lord commands.'

Carla began to feel annoyed with her. Why couldn't she stop? The blonde must be insane — the doctor had no right to confine her in the same room. She'd complain about it.

Meanwhile, she had to lie there and listen. It seemed to go on for hours, then —

A key grated in the lock of the steel door. The door opened and a man came in. He was dressed in white like a hospital orderly. Carla thought: they ought to have female nurses.

He was a broad, tough-looking man with a battered face.

'So you've come round,' he said, looking at Carla. 'About time too.'

Carla said: 'I'm all right now. I'm not mad. I demand to see the doctor.'

The male nurse took no notice of her. He pulled back the bedclothes and unfastened the metal band round her ankle.

'Get up,' he grunted. 'You're to take a bath. Doctor Arnaud is coming to see you and he likes his patients to be bathed before he touches them.'

Carla flared up: 'I *am* clean! I want to see the doctor now!'

He pushed her out through the door and locked it behind him.

'To save you worrying,' he said. 'The doors at each end of the passage are locked. You can't get out, so don't try.'

Carla looked down the white-walled corridor. There was an impressive steel door at each end. She didn't try to run.

The man marched her along the passage and unlocked another door. Beyond it was the bathroom. He ran hot water and said:

'Strip, baby!'

Carla glared at him.

'Not with you here,' she retorted.

The man sneered at her.

'Don't worry about me, baby.'

Carla defied him.

'I won't undress,' she said. 'I *demand* to see the doctor!'

The man grunted and grabbed hold of her. He dragged her to the bath and shoved her head under water, holding her down until she went limp. Carla gurgled, choking. She began to black out. He hauled her out again and slapped her face till she came to.

'No arguments,' he said, 'or you'll get the same again. Now, strip — and wash yourself!'

Carla sucked down air into her lungs. She panted with fury.

'I'll report you to the doctor,' she snapped. 'You can't treat patients like that.'

He laughed.

'This is a very special kind of a hospital. A sanatorium — a nut-house. The doc knows we have to rough you a little, so it won't do you any good to cry about it.'

Carla turned her back on him while she took off her jacket She dropped her pyjama trousers and plunged into the water and began washing herself. The male nurse leaned against the wall, smoking and watching her.

'He sure knows how to pick 'em,' he grunted. 'I get tired of seeing so much beauty. Come on, hurry it up — we ain't got all day.'

Carla got out of the bath and took the towel he handed her She dried herself and stepped into the pyjamas.

'Where are my own clothes?' she demanded.

The male nurse grinned.

'Baby, when you were delivered here, all you had on were panties and stockings and brassiere. Very nice too — I gave the stuff to a cute little blonde I know. She looks swell in black net!'

Carla's eyes blazed — to think that this brute had undressed her . . . she shuddered. He took her back to the cell where the other girl was still muttering to herself. Carla got back into bed and watched him fasten the ankle band again. She bit her lip.

'Do I have to have *that* on?' she wanted to know.

'Sure baby — you nuts get wild at times!'

'I'm not crazy,' Carla said, 'I'm *not!*'

She said it again, calmly. It suddenly seemed very important to convince this man that she was sane.

'I'm perfectly all right,' she insisted.

'Sure baby — I know.'

He leaned against the door waiting. When he heard the sound of the far passage door opening he ground out his cigarette and straightened up.

'Now, no trouble now or I'll get rough. The doc's coming.'

Doctor Arnaud was a dapper man with a neat moustache. He came in briskly, carrying a case that he gave to the male nurse. All his movements were brisk. He seemed like a man who had to go somewhere in a hurry.

'All ready, Jordan?' he asked.

'She's had her bath — looked swell too.'

'Shapirro likes them that way,' Dr. Arnaud remarked.

Shapirro!

Carla shot up in bed with a startled cry. At the sound of the name, her memory came back. It was like a key turning in a lock. She remembered everything. Her father. King. The twins. Piggot — she'd killed him. And the crazy house with the black-and-white motif and Sylvester Shapirro and his strange desires and lovely

114

girls. She remembered Phyllis — and Shapirro doping her.

Dr. Arnaud looked at her sharply.

'It's come back, eh? Queer how the dope affects some girls more than others.' Carla didn't know whether he was speaking to her, Jordan, or muttering to himself. 'Some girls go under quickly — some have to have the stuff pumped into them for months. But it drains them all in time.'

'Let me out of here,' Carla pleaded. 'I don't want to be like the others. I don't — '

Jordan hit her across the mouth, knocking her flat.

'Shaddup!' he growled.

Dr. Arnaud opened the case and took out a hypodermic. He filled it with professional quickness.

'Hold her down, Jordan — I'll give her another shot now.'

Carla tried to get away. She came off the bed in a hurry, forgetting the chain round her ankle. Stabbing pain shot through her leg and she fell flat on her face. Jordan picked her up and slung her back on the bed.

Carla began to struggle as he rolled up her sleeve. She bit his hand. Jordan swore and hit her brutally.

'You little bitch! Keep still or I'll really hurt you!'

He kneeled across her, pinning her with his weight, twisting her arms so that every movement she made was agonizing torture. Carla moaned with pain. She saw Dr. Arnaud coming towards her, hypodermic in hand, smiling. She began to scream.

Jordan stuffed a handful of blanket into her month, choking her. She lay there, quivering with fear, tears streaming down her cheeks while Jordan held her down. She felt the coldness of antiseptic on her arm — the faint prick of the needle as Dr. Arnaud searched for the vein. Then the dope was going into her — pumping into her, making her crazy with terror. Her arm throbbed cruelly as the liquid surged in . . .

Carla's head felt as if it were bursting. She was one pounding dynamo, throbbing violently. Her heart thumped louder

— louder. She didn't feel the needle come out.

She was falling through space. Spiralling down into a lightless void. A black suffocating sludge swamped her consciousness, sucking her into oblivion — blotting out the agony, the fear, everything. She drifted into sleep . . .

★   ★   ★

The light hurt her eyes again. Her arm was stiff. The metal band hurt her ankle as she moved her leg. Memory returned as she heard the blonde talking to herself —

'I must do as my lord commands . . .' Over and over.

Carla struggled up in bed and snarled at the blonde:

'Stop it! For God's sake — stop it!'

Jordan looked in through the grille in the steel door. He grinned at her.

'Don't let it get you down, baby — you'll be like that one day!'

He came in, a few minutes later, with a tray of food.

'Eat up, baby — chicken, eggs, salad, milk. We look after our patients here. Shapirro doesn't like his lovelies to pine away.'

Carla wanted to hurl the tray at him, but the food tempted her. Saliva formed in her mouth. She felt as if she hadn't eaten for weeks. And, if she were to escape, she had to keep up her strength. She ate ravenously.

She tried to blot out the incessant muttering of the blonde in the next bed. Tried not to think of the dope already in her body — at least it hadn't affected her mind yet. She could still think clearly, still remember Sylvester Shapirro, still hate! Hate boiled up inside her like a living thing. She wanted to get Shapirro in a corner and kill him, slowly, painfully.

Jordan took away the empty tray and left her alone with the blonde. Carla tried to talk to her; to make her stop muttering, but it was no use. The blonde was too far gone.

Carla wondered how long it would be before the blonde was taken away to the house with the black-and-white motif, to become a plaything of an old man with white hair and pink eyes.

She tried to think how she could escape. She had to get the chain off her ankle, get the door unlocked. Then there were the steel doors at the end of the corridor. And after that? Her hopes began to sink . . . if only King would come. But he didn't know where to find her. Nobody knew where to look for her.

Jordan took her for a bath. She looked at the nurse thoughtfully. Maybe . . .

She swayed towards him, inviting him with her eyes. Her arms went out —

'I can be very nice to a man,' she said softly. 'You'd like me, wouldn't you?'

She leaned forward, watching the way he looked at her licking his lips.

'If you got me out of here,' she whispered, 'we could go away together — just you and me . . .'

Jordan pushed her off. He laughed harshly.

'Forget it, baby. Shapirro would carve me into little pieces if I even kissed you — you haven't a hope of getting out of this joint. Not a hope!'

Carla gave up. She took her bath and went back to the tiny cell where the blonde talked all the time in a dull monotone. Jordan chained her to the bed again. Then Dr. Arnaud came with his hypodermic to shoot more dope into her — and Carla blacked out for the third time.

She had no idea how long she'd been unconscious; no idea of time at all. Days might have passed since she entered the sanatorium. Or weeks. Or only hours. She had no way of telling.

Always, there was Jordan to bathe her, to feed her, to chain her again. And the blonde muttering in the other bed. And Dr. Arnaud with his hypodermic. There was a cycle to her existence, a cycle of sleeping and waking while they waited for the dope to break down her resistance. But Carla clung on with hate in her heart. Hope had gone — there was only hate now.

Once, she tried to escape. She was returning from the bathroom, Jordan behind her, when the far door of the corridor opened. Dr. Arnaud came in, carrying his case.

Carla went crazy. She sprinted down the passage, screaming with the full power of her lungs. She had to get through that door before the doctor locked it. Jordan ran after her, swearing violently. She reached the door and clawed at the doctor with her nails, leaving red weals on his face. He staggered back — and Carla darted for the door.

She had a glimpse of a long hall leading onto a green lawn. She saw the blue sky outside — freedom! Then Dr Arnaud stuck out his foot, tripping her. Before she could recover, Jordan leapt on her, beating her to the ground with his fists.

The male nurse dragged her along the passage by her hair, kicking her. He threw her on the bed, chained her ankle.

'You'd better punish her, Jordan,' said the doctor. 'She must be taught the futility of attempting to escape.'

Jordan growled and went out of the cell. Dr. Arnaud wiped his bleeding face and glared at Carla. She tried to wriggle away, frightened, but the chain held her prisoner.

Jordan came back with a straightjacket. He grabbed hold of Carla and forced her arms into the straightjacket, wrapping it round her. He knelt on top of her, squeezing the air out of her lungs, tightening the cord laces brutally. When he'd finished, Carla was in excruciating agony. Her arms were lashed behind her, stretched almost to breaking point; the jacket was so tight she could hardly breathe. It was an effort, a slow, painful effort to even half-fill her lungs with air.

'A couple of hours in that will cool you off,' Jordan growled. 'You won't try to get away again!'

They left her like that. Carla moaned for a while; she soon stopped moaning because it hurt so much — it took up more air than she could get into her lungs. She concentrated on breathing — she had to concentrate, it was that difficult.

She lay there in racking pain, her brain going slowly numb, her body losing its power. And all the while, she had to listen to the blonde repeating her grim text:

'I must do as my lord commands . . . I must do as my lord commands.'

When Dr. Arnaud and Jordan came back, Carla was nearly unconscious. The nurse took off the straightjacket and wiped her arm with antiseptic. She hadn't the power to raise her arm or utter a cry of protest. The doctor jabbed in the needle and Carla passed out.

Jordan laughed as he looked down at her. He said:

'*She* won't last much longer — she's ready to crack!'

9

Dawn was a redness in the morning air when King Logan reached Mount Vernon. He turned into the drive leading up to the home of Matthew Bowman. His legs ached; his feet were blistered. He was a hunted man, desperate, looking for cover. He wanted time to think, to rest, to form a new gang — then he was going after Shapirro.

King went in by a side window. There seemed to be no one about as he padded cautiously along the ground floor passages. He took out his gun and caressed it lovingly. His stubbled face cracked in a grim smile — if anyone offered trouble, that would be just too bad for them.

He found the larder and ate some bread and cheese. There was a crate of beer and he drank a couple of bottles, wiping his mouth with the back of his hand. He felt better, and set off on a tour of inspection. In the servants' quarters, he found the butler still in bed.

He went through the house, room by room. There were no other servants. Matthew Bowman's wants were few and the butler attended to them. Carla wasn't at home — he found her bedroom and looked in eagerly. He was disappointed.

He heard Old Matthew's snores and woke him.

'Where's Carla?' King demanded, prodding the old man with his gun.

Matthew Bowman tried to sit up. King hit him, bringing on a severe heart attack. He lay back, gasping for air, holding his chest. King laughed, and hit him again.

'You ain't got the stamina your daughter has!' he jeered.

Bowman's attack subsided. He glared at King.

'Who are you?' he snapped. 'And what do you know about Carla?'

'Carla!' King chuckled. 'What *don't* I know! I'm King Logan — I don't suppose she told you about me — you might call me her husband, though we've never been legally married — if you get my meaning!'

Old Matthew's face went red. He spluttered with rage.

'You cheap hoodlum! Get out of my house — I'll call the police — I'll — '

King slapped him across the face with the flat of his gun.

'You won't do nothin', old man,' he jeered. 'Your butler's asleep — and we're alone in the house. Just the two of us! Now, where's Carla?'

'I don't know — and if I did I wouldn't tell you!'

Matthew Bowman glared at King. It couldn't be true, not Carla and this — this brute! He refused to believe it. He stared at King Logan's six feet of muscle, his dark, close-cropped hair and beady eyes. The missing finger on his right hand gave him a sinister air; his brutal manner and the gun he carried told Bowman all he wanted to know about King. Carla couldn't have been such a fool . . .

King guessed his thoughts and laughed.

'Yeah, she's mine all right.' He licked his lips. 'Carla's sure a swell baby!'

Matthew Bowman's parchment face wrinkled with disgust. His faded eyes sparked with fury. He shook a gnarled hand at King.

'Don't dare speak of my daughter like that!' he rasped, his voice quavering.

He slumped back, gasping, clutching his heart again.

'I guess you ain't long for this world,' King said coldly. 'I guess — '

He broke off as a telephone bell shrilled through the room. They both looked at the phone. Bowman tried to reach it but King pushed him back suspiciously.

'I don't think we'll answer that,' he grunted. 'Let it ring.'

The phone shrilled out, again and again. Matthew Bowman wanted to answer it. He said:

'Carla! It must be Carla. I want to talk to her. I must see her again, before — '
He slumped back, gasping with pain. 'Before — it's too late,' he finished.

'Yeah,' said King thoughtfully, 'it might be Carla.'

He picked up the receiver and answered it, carefully disguising his voice:

'Mr. Bowman's home. The butler speaking.'

A faint whisper came back, sending a shiver of fear through King's spine.

'This is Sylvester Shapirro. I want to speak to Matthew Bowman in person. Tell him I have news of his daughter.'

King's face went hard. Maybe Jerry had been right — maybe Carla was double-crossing him. If she were . . .

He pushed the phone into Old Matthew's gnarled hand, and hissed:

'Answer it. One word out of turn and I'll put a slug between your eyes!'

He jammed the muzzle of his .45 against Bowman's high forehead and bent to overhear the conversation. He had to know what Shapirro wanted, to know if Carla had double-crossed him.

The whispered voice that came back froze the blood in his veins. Shapirro said:

'I think you ought to know the truth about your daughter. She's a nymphomaniac — a killer. She was going about with a gang-leader called King Logan. She murdered the detective, Piggot, you sent after her. And now she has been committed to a sanatorium for the insane . . . '

The phone dropped from Old Matthew's shaking hand. Carla! His heart thumped madly; his frail body shook. He doubled up in swift recurring convulsions. The shock had been too much for Matthew Bowman. In fifteen seconds, he lay stretched out in death. Never again would he worry over his erring daughter.

Slowly, King Logan replaced the receiver on its hook. He didn't look at the contorted face of Matthew Bowman. He was thinking about Sylvester Shapirro — how did he know where Carla was? Carla *wasn't* insane — King knew that. Why had Shapirro lied about her? Unless . . .

If Carla had double-crossed him and gone to Shapirro, then he would want to cover up for her. Jerry had been right, after all — she *had* ratted on him. King swore horribly and his hand tightened about the butt of his automatic.

He'd get Shapirro and Carla . . . he'd get her like he'd said he would!

★ ★ ★

Eddie Gifford sat in Martha Franks' downtown Manhattan apartment facing

129

her. The woman's pale face was deeply lined and her hands shook: the black dress made her appear a grim and forbidding figure despite her slightness. Her faded eyes were bleak, hiding the emptiness she felt deep down inside.

'So you can't get anything on William's murderer,' she said bitterly.

Eddie shrugged.

'Not so far. Shapirro's clever — all the dirty work is done by others — he makes sure nothing can lead back to him. As for Logan, he's still hiding out somewhere. And I can't find Carla to get a lead on him. Old Bowman doesn't know where she is.' He paused.

'I feel sorry for Bowman. He's worried stiff about his daughter and, in his condition, he's likely to kick the bucket any time he really learns what she's been up to. Carla's wild, all right — wild as an untamed tiger. I suppose she's with Logan, wherever he is.'

Martha said: 'I want you to get to Shapirro — somehow.'

Eddie nodded.

'I've been thinking about it. I guess I'll

have to try another line. The Bowery's quiet these days — the shopkeepers pay up and don't make any trouble; Shapirro gets it all his own way without Logan to give him competition. And the Waldemar twins, Shapirro's kingpins, aren't around East Side much. They leave it all to their hatchet men. But — '

Eddie reflected, before continuing:

'But there's another angle. Shapirro, so the rumour goes, has a fancy for young girls. From time to time, a beautiful young girl simply disappears from New York. Usually, nothing is done about it because the girl has no parents or friends to take action. Shapirro picks them carefully, but he picks them. And eventually they must end up at Montauk Point.'

Martha frowned, and said:

'Maybe that's where Carla is?'

'I hadn't thought of that,' Eddie admitted. He brooded over the point. 'I don't see that it helps us much anyway — though I might mention it to Matthew Bowman. He might stir the cops into activity if I can sell him that idea. In any case, the girls usually disappear from the ritzy nightclubs on West Side. Glamour girls with a swell figure and no one to worry about them — if anyone does notice they're not around any more, it's assumed they've found themselves a sugar-daddy. And Shapirro's name isn't mentioned.'

Eddie got to his feet.

'There's the *Paradise Club* on Riverside Drive — that's where the Waldemar twins operate from. I'm going there to keep an eye on things and, if I can get proof that the twins kidnap girls for Shapirro, I may be able to get the G-men interested. And once I can get them investigating maybe we can pin murder on the man who killed your husband.'

Martha's eyes lit up. She clenched her fragile hands.

'That's right! That's what I want — make Shapirro pay with his own life. You get him for me, Eddie!'

Eddie said: 'I'll get him!'

He went down the three flights of wooden stairs and out into the dingy street. It was still light, too early for visiting the nightclubs on West Side. He drove to a bar off Broadway and ate a couple of ham sandwiches in between ryes. The more he thought about his coming trip to the *Paradise Club*, the more certain he felt that he'd get a lead there — a lead that would give him something definite on Sylvester Shapirro.

★   ★   ★

The black glass walls of the room seemed to recede to infinity. Concealed tubes threw a soft light over the old man seated behind the transparent plastic desk. The mop of snow-white hair was sharply etched against the black drape behind Sylvester Shapirro; the tiny pink eyes were bright in his wrinkled face.

Shapirro replaced the telephone and smiled at the Waldemar twins. His voice was an eerie whisper that echoed from the walls.

'I don't think we shall be bothered by Matthew Bowman. Not now.' He chuckled softly. 'His heart wasn't strong enough to stand the shock of learning the truth

133

about his daughter — and now no one will be interested in finding out exactly where she is.'

Rufus Waldemar swished his cane. His handsome face impassive, his twin blue eyes cold as he replied:

'Except King Logan.'

Shapirro frowned. He picked up the whip on his desk and played with the lash.

'Logan must be found,' he said. 'He must be exterminated.'

Glenn Waldemar moved uneasily. His oddly coloured eyes shifted to the ebony coffin in the alcove. He said:

'But where is he? You can't kill a man you can't find.'

'We'll find him,' Shapirro whispered. 'He can't remain under cover indefinitely. I've men all over New York watching for him — as soon as he reveals himself, he'll be picked up. Then you can take care of him — permanently!'

He, too, looked towards the empty coffin. He sighed.

'Joe Mazzini took such trouble with his coffin, too. It would be a pity to waste Joe's talent — Logan must die. We'll give him a wonderful burial, with no expense spared. It'll be a lesson for any other budding gang-leaders not to encroach on my territory. And now, let us forget Logan. There are more pressing considerations.'

The Waldemar twins waited. Shapirro flicked the long lash with his hand, cracking it in the air.

'Rufus,' he whispered, 'there's a private detective named Eddie Gifford sticking his nose into our affairs. He's employed by the widow of one of the men we had to remove suddenly. Her name is Mrs. Franks and she has a room in an apartment house in Manhattan. You'll take care of her.'

He paused, cracked the whip again.

'Gifford will have to be handled more carefully. Although he's a private agent, he's in good standing with the police. Something subtle will have to be used on Mr. Gifford. You might try persuading him to mind his own business. Just a warning — but impress on him the urgency of the warning. Next time he'll end up in the Hudson. I think you might use Gringold — he's a useful man for such a case.'

Rufus slicked back his blond hair and swished his gold-tipped cane.

'I'll attend to it at once,' he said, and left the room.

Shapirro's pink eyes settled on Glenn Waldemar.

'Dr. Arnaud has another girl ready for me. A blonde. I want you to go out to the sanatorium and bring her back with you. While you're there, you can enquire how Carla is. I'm very keen to include Carla in my harem — you might suggest that the doctor hurries her treatment a little. That's all.'

Glenn Waldemar went out of the room. He'd forgotten all about Carla, the lovely girl with the black hair and dark eyes. She'd been nice — he'd have liked to play around with Carla, but Shapirro didn't like anyone touching his girls. Glenn Waldemar scowled. Maybe something could happen to Carla before she was ready for the house at Montauk Point. Maybe . . . his eyes glowed as he thought about that. If he worked it right, Shapirro need never know . . .

Alone in the room with the black-and-white motif, Sylvester Shapirro pressed a button on his desk. One of the black glass walls changed, became transparent. He looked through into the other room, watching the drugged girls who posed for him.

His pink eyes rested on a brunette. She was a magnificently built girl with long wavy hair. She crouched, doubled up in a baby's cot, her long legs pressed against the wooden bars. Her only covering was a white, woolly diaper round her hips, fastened with an outsize safety pin.

Shapirro chuckled as he looked at the girl. He pressed another button on his desk and chimes sounded. He spoke into a hidden microphone:

'Come to your lord, Iris. Come quickly, he wants to nurse his beautiful baby . . . '

The girl climbed out of her cot, stiffly, and walked towards the door. Her face was empty of expression; she moved like an automaton. As she came up to him, Shapirro picked up his whip and cracked the lash. He smiled as the tip of the lash stroked her body, leaving a red weal across the white skin.

Iris shuddered. Her body quivered uncontrollably and a look of fear came to her eyes. But she didn't move away. She stood there, waiting . . . the hideous drug had broken her spirit.

Shapirro flicked the lash again, and chuckled. He might be an old man; he might not take his pleasures in the usual way — but he got a lot of fun out of his harem. Oh, yes, Sylvester Shapirro knew how to enjoy himself!

10

Everything was the same. First came the grey mist, the blinding light; then the tugging at her ankle. The walls of the room were padded with rubber-sponge and the blonde in the other bed still talked to herself.

Carla had to force herself to remember things. She knew the drug was dulling her brain, reducing her to a will-less body. A shell without a personality. She fought it. She clung to life with her burning hatred. She lay there, thinking of Shapirro, hating him, and forcing her mind back to reality, with thoughts of revenge. She planned slow, horrible deaths for the old man with pink eyes.

The door of the cell opened and Jordan came in. Carla sat up, her mind clearing as she saw the debonair figure of Rufus Waldemar follow him in. She recognized the handsome face, the blond hair, the blue eyes . . . no, one was brown. It was

Glenn Waldemar.

Jordan went over to the blonde and turned back the bedclothes. He unlocked the metal band round her ankle. The blonde took no notice; she simply said:

'I must do as my lord commands . . . '

Over and over, in a flat monotone.

'Stand up,' Jordan said.

The blonde got off the bed and stood motionless while Jordan dressed her. He took away the coarse linen pyjamas and inspected her with the air of a connoisseur.

'Shapirro will like this one,' he said. 'She's ready for him — not an ounce of spirit left in her.' She didn't move, didn't show the slightest emotion. Jordan added: 'Personally, I prefer a dame with some spirit.'

Glenn was looking at Carla. He said:

'Me. too!'

Carla felt a tiny flutter of hope. She remembered how Glenn had kissed her the night she'd shot Piggot. He'd wanted her then . . . if she could interest him now, maybe . . .

She wasn't wearing much under the

pyjamas and Glenn's eyes lit up as he saw the dark swell rise and fall with her breathing. Carla flashed him a provocative look, tempting him. Glenn licked his lips and took a step towards her. Remembering Jordan, he checked himself. He looked at Carla in a meaningful way ... Carla felt exultant. He was hooked — she knew Glenn wouldn't leave her alone now. He'd be back, all right.

Jordan hadn't seen their little byplay; he was still regarding the blonde.

He chucked her pyjamas into the corridor.

'You won't need those any more, sister — where you're going, you'll get fancy clothes to wear.' He chuckled. 'Very fancy!'

Glenn said: 'Can't you make her stop muttering? It's getting on my nerves. I'm not driving her back to Montauk Point while she's going on like that.'

'Easy,' said Jordan confidently. 'We've got her trained.' He snapped at the blonde: 'Stop talking!'

She did. It was like a radio set switched

off. Carla shuddered. The silence was frightening. So used had she become to the blonde's unceasing voice that the abrupt silence scared her. It made her realize how completely the doped girl was under their control. And one day, unless she escaped, she'd be like that.

Glenn took the girl's arm and led her out into the passage. He shot another glance at Carla in passing. She smiled quietly. Oh yes, Glenn would be back!

After they'd gone, Jordan turned to Carla.

'You're awake, are you?' He looked at her curiously. 'Still remembering things?'

Carla said: 'Yes, I remember . . . and one day I'm going to pay you out for everything you've done to me.'

Jordan laughed.

'Forget it, baby! The doc will be here in a few minutes. Shapirro wants you in a hurry — we've orders to speed up your treatment.'

Carla shivered in sudden fear. Surely, they couldn't do anything worse to her?

'We've never had to double the dose before,' Jordan said. He looked at her critically, almost professionally. 'Maybe you won't live through it. Funny stuff, this dope — can't rely on it at all.'

Carla's mouth went dry, her heart pounding furiously. She wouldn't die — she wouldn't let Shapirro win. She'd hang on somehow, live on her hate. Hang on till Glenn came back, then she'd escape. Already, she was planning it . . .

'Does Glenn Waldemar come often?' she asked, trying to seem casual.

Jordan was in a talkative mood. Maybe getting rid of the blonde made him feel better. He said:

'Not often. He used to be here all the time, him and Rufus. They were the only genuine patients we ever had — crazy as coots, both of 'em — that was before Shapirro took over. Doctor Arnaud was on the wrong side of the medical council and Shapirro found out. He started blackmailing him — and me! Shapirro took a fancy to the Waldemar twins. Psychopaths they are — killers. Shapirro knew he could use a couple of boys like that so he got Arnaud to turn them over to his care — and he lets 'em out to bump off any guys who get in his way!'

Carla felt her blood freeze. Glenn was mad — a killer!

She wondered if she'd be able to control him. If he had a fit, took it into his head to kill her . . . She blocked out the thought.

'Then Shapirro started bringing girls here to be doped. We couldn't say 'no' — not with Shapirro threatening us. That's how it's been ever since.'

Jordan looked at Carla and grinned.

'But it won't worry you much longer — you'll be the same way as the blonde in a few days. Or dead!'

Doctor Arnaud came in with his case. He took out the hypodermic and filled it.

Jordan said: 'Now, take it easy sister. No use fretting. Take your shot like a little lady and I won't twist your arms off.'

He held her down while the doctor rolled up her sleeve; and dabbed antiseptic on her arm. Carla watched the needle coming nearer. She tried to relax. She knew it was no use struggling, but she couldn't just lie there and let them fill her full of dope. She couldn't take it in cold blood.

She tried to crawl away, to get out of reach of Dr. Arnaud. Jordan cursed her. He twisted her arms till she screamed with pain, then hit her across the mouth with his fist. Carla lay in a quivering heap, helpless.

She felt the needle pierce her skin; moaned as the dope pumped into her veins, mingling with her blood. It seemed to go on for longer than usual and she guessed that the doctor was feeding her a double dose of the stuff. Her arm seemed to swell as the liquid throbbed through her body. Her head pounded: the walls started to dance crazily and the light grew dim.

She was falling into a black pit, turning head over heels.

Consciousness began to fade. A moist, suffocating blanket smothered her. It was getting darker, darker . . . then there was nothing. No pain. No light. No hate. Nothing.

★ ★ ★

Eddie drove slowly along Broadway, watching the bright lights and feeling a little sick at the crime that ran unchecked beneath the surface of the big city. It was night, but you'd never have known. Looking up between the towering buildings, the sky was ablaze with neon signs. It was brighter than day.

He turned off on West 86th Street and picked up speed on Riverside Drive. The river was quiet and dark, though the lights of New Jersey, across the water, made a glittering backdrop to the velvet night. Here, by the river, it was possible to see the stars in the heavens, despite the glare of artificial light.

Eddie's car moved swiftly along Riverside Drive, to the *Paradise Club*. He parked the car and went into the club.

As he walked up to the bar, his eyes moved round the tables searching for the Waldemar twins. They didn't appear to be present.

He sat on a stool by the bar, sipping rye and smoking.

The cabaret started. The girls were briefly attired and a great success with the male patrons of the club. Eddie brooded, wondering if one of the showgirls was slated for Shapirro's home. It was something Eddie wouldn't have wanted to happen to someone he cared about. He'd heard tales of Sylvester Shapirro — none of them pleasant.

The evening wore on. The tables began to fill. Eddie sat drinking, waiting — then, the Waldemar twins came in.

He'd never seen them before, but he recognized them instantly from descriptions he'd been given.

They sauntered into the club, cool, debonair, swinging their gold-tipped canes. He studied them closely. They were both extremely handsome, both dressed quietly in grey suits; their blond hair glinted under the bright light. Their faces were smiling; cold, deadly smiles that masked strange emotions. Rufus's eyes were both blue; Glenn had one blue and one brown eye, which gave him a sinister cast. It was the only apparent difference.

The twins ordered drinks and sat there, not speaking, just sipping from the tall cone-shaped glasses, idly looking round the club. Glenn's eyes glittered as he watched the cabaret girls; Rufus showed no interest in them. That told Eddie they weren't so much alike as they looked. He began to wonder about them.

Rufus's twin blue eyes settled briefly on Eddie, and passed on. Glenn didn't look his way; he was too busy; staring at the lovely girls parading their charms for all to see. Eddie sank another rye and moved to a less conspicuous position. He didn't think Rufus Waldemar knew who he was, but he didn't want those sharp blue eyes settling on him again. Eddie preferred to remain incognito.

He took up a position at a table by the wall, in shadow, screened by a purple drape that half-covered a secluded nook. From there, he could watch the twins without being seen by them. He sat and waited.

Rufus's attention was suddenly caught by a man and a girl in one of the corner scats. He nudged his brother's arm and nodded his head. Glenn stared at the couple. He smiled. Eddie saw Rufus whisper something to him, and Glenn got up and left the table. Rufus continued to sit alone, hardly taking his eyes off the pair in the corner.

Eddie couldn't see them very well from his position, and he didn't want to reveal his interest in Glenn Waldemar by changing his seat, so he waited. But now he was tensed.

Something was about to happen — he was sure of that.

It was a quarter of an hour later when the couple left the corner seat. Eddie took a good look at them. The man was about forty, well-dressed, flashing an expensive jewelled tie-pin. He looked like a prosperous businessman out for a good time — and the girl looked the sort to give it to him.

She was, perhaps, twenty, with exciting red hair and a slim, willowy figure. She wore a revealing evening dress, and one of the shoulder straps had slipped a little.

They passed Eddie's table, on the way out. The redhead's face was flushed and she giggled; she'd had too much to drink. The man's arm was about her waist, half-supporting her. Eddie didn't have much trouble in guessing that the elderly man had propositioned her for the night . . . or that she'd accepted for the hard cash she'd get out of him.

He saw Rufus Waldemar follow them out of the club.

Eddie paid his check and hurried after Waldemar. He had a notion something was due to happen to the redhead, and he wanted to be on hand when it did. But the quickness of the action took him by surprise and he was too late to stop the killing.

Eddie arrived at the door leading onto the car park as the man and girl reached a car. A shadow glided from behind the car. Moonlight gleamed on Glenn Waldemar's blond hair, on the cold, cruel expression of his face, on the steel blade that shot from his gold-tipped cane. He struck savagely, thrusting the steel into the elderly man's stomach, twisting it.

The man fell in a heap, holding his stomach, groaning. Rufus Waldemar hit the redhead on the back of her head before she could scream. Between them, they dragged her into a large black Rolls.

The powerful car surged forward, out of the park, as Eddie ran forward.

Eddie was sweating. His scalp prickled with fear. Never had he seen such a cold-blooded, deliberate murder. The twins had planned it to a fraction of a second — and they were away with the girl. Another nymph for Shapirro to play with. The kidnapping had taken Eddie completely by surprise, so swiftly, so smoothly had it been carried out.

He reached the man and bent over him. Eddie knew it was too late to help him. He was dying fast. Eddie sprinted for his own car and drove after the Rolls with reckless speed. He wanted to know where the twins were taking the kidnapped girl; wanted them to lead him to Sylvester Shapirro.

The Rolls was moving fast, tearing up Riverside Drive, heading north. There was little traffic about and Eddie drove without lights, not wanting the twins to see they were being followed. He watched the red tail light ahead and clung to it.

The Rolls swung right at West 155th Street and crossed the Harlem River by

Macombs Bridge. It streaked down Jerome Avenue then up Grand Boulevard and Concourse, kept to the centre of the concrete strip, heading north, out of the Bronx.

Eddie was puzzled because the car wasn't aiming at Long Island and Shapirro's house on Montauk Point; then he realized that Shapirro was too cunning to have the girl taken direct to him. There would be a reception point somewhere, and the girl would be doped before being moved to Long Island. Eddie watched the red tail light, grimly determined to learn where Shapirro's girls were treated. With that information, he thought he'd be able to set the forces of law and order in motion.

Eddie had his foot hard down on the accelerator, driving it into the floorboards. The speedometer needle hovered around eighty; even then, he only just managed to keep the Rolls in sight. He prayed that the Waldemar's car was going flat out.

The Rolls crossed the State line and roared on. Eddie followed. The two cars streaked through the deserted countryside. It was dark now, beyond the city lights. The moon bathed the hills in silver light. Ahead lay Connecticut.

Eddie realized he was driving through Phoenix Springs, the tiny state wedged between New York and Connecticut.

A crossroads loomed ahead. Eddie cursed, and tried to use his brakes as the nose of a patrol car swung out into the road. He grazed it, careered crazily along the road, scraping the hedge. Branches lashed the windows the bonnet of the car rammed a tree and came to an abrupt halt. Eddie jerked forward, hitting his head on the dashboard, shaking him up.

He opened the door and staggered out. His legs weren't working property and his eyes hazed over. He stared along the road; the tail light of the Rolls was no longer in view.

The patrol car Eddie had nearly rammed pulled ahead, blocking the road. Two uniformed cops got out. They were accompanied by a man in brown.

One of the cops pulled out a flask and offered Eddie a drink. He gulped it down, his head clearing rapidly. He knew only one thing — he had to get after the black Rolls fast.

He pulled out his private investigator's badge and flashed it to the cops.

'We've got to get after that car,' he said urgently. 'The two men in it have just committed murder. They're getting away with a kidnapped girl!'

The cop who had given Eddie the drink laughed. He was a thickset man with a long face.

'Ya hear that, Louis?' he said to the other cop. 'This guy's a private dick and he was chasing kidnappers — just like the films, ain't it?'

'Yeah,' growled Louis, a broad-shouldered cop with hands the size of hams, 'I hear him. You wouldn't think we were cops at all, would yuh? You wouldn't think this guy was encroaching on our territory, would yuh?'

The man in brown came up. He had a fat paunch and red face with an unpleasant expression. His eyes glinted.

'A private snoop from the big city, huh?' he said flatly. 'These New York dicks come barging in, thinking they can run everything. They make me tired!'

Eddie was losing his temper.

'Listen,' he growled. 'I want to get after that Rolls!'

Louis put a massive fist to his chest and pushed him. Eddie staggered back against his car, hitting his head. There was a mist before his eyes and he couldn't see clearly.

'Look at him, Buck,' Louis jeered. 'Staggering. Drunk, so he is! Driving under the influence of alcohol.'

Buck hauled Eddie upright and held him still.

'Smell his breath, chief,' he invited.

The man in brown sniffed.

'Yeah,' he said. 'He's drunk all right. Maybe we'd better beat him up a little — can't have dangerous driving in Phoenix Springs.'

Buck held Eddie while Louis hit him. Eddie winced and tried to get away.

'Ya see that?' Buck said. 'Resisting arrest!'

'You lousy coppers!' Eddie snarled. 'I'll get — '

Louis hit him again. Eddie didn't fall because Buck was still holding him; he swayed on his feet.

'Ya hear that?' Buck said. 'Insulting the police!'

The man in brown stepped closer. He said:

'Listen, Gifford, we know all about you. We've been expecting you, see? And we don't like private dicks in Phoenix Springs. I'm Gringold, Chief of Police for this state, and I don't want you around. Do I make myself clear?'

'Yeah,' Eddie snarled. 'It's clear enough. How much does Shapirro pay you?'

Gringold smiled coldly.

'Shapirro's a very good friend of mine. And he doesn't want you sticking your nose in his private business. We're giving you a little warning, that's all.'

Buck twisted Eddie's arms behind him. Louis got out a nightstick and spat on it. He raised it, ready to strike.

Eddie kicked Buck's shins, ducking sideways as the stick came down. It missed his skull, landed on his shoulder with stunning force. He moaned and staggered back. Louis came after him. He slammed down the nightstick again, on Eddie's other shoulder.

Eddie moaned a little. The pain in his shoulders prevented him raising his arms to protect himself. He had to stand there and take it.

Gringold said: 'We could book you for a night in the cells. Drunk while driving. Resisting arrest. Insulting the force. But I don't like wasting the taxpayers' money on a heel like you — so we'll just give you a beating and turn you loose. But don't let me catch you in Phoenix Springs again. Next time, you won't get off so lightly.'

Buck hit Eddie at the base of the spine and let him fall forward, Louis brought up his knee, ramming it hard into Eddie's groin. Eddie fell flat on his face and lay writhing on the ground. He felt sick with pain.

Buck and Louis started to kick him around. They wore heavy boots, studded with nails. Eddie tried to cover his face. They kicked him in the stomach. Eddie brought down his arms . . . a boot slammed into his mouth, Eddie spat out blood and choked on a loose tooth. They went on kicking him, brutally, viciously.

His arms hung loosely. His legs were bruised so badly he couldn't even crawl away. His spine throbbed; his stomach felt as if it would never hold anything again.

He was blacking out. The mists were closing in, swamping him. He heard Gringold's voice:

'Keep out of Shapirro's way, Gifford. Keep your nose clean — next time, you'll end up on a slab in the morgue!'

A heavy boot crashed into Eddie's skull. He shuddered, rolled over. The pain was going away and, with it, his consciousness. The darkness came in waves, beating over him like surf on the shore. The waves piled up on him, carrying him down to the bottom of a dark sea where it was cool and quiet, and no longer did he feel the agony of his tortured body.

11

If only Glenn would come . . .

Carla lay on the bed, awake again. But only half awake. The grey mist never went completely away now. The walls were a little hazy, the light in the ceiling seemed a long way off.

She knew the drug was taking effect, beating down her resistance, reducing her to a will-less automaton. Soon, she would be helpless, a living zombie to carry out Shapirro's orders. The metal band round her ankle was a dull ache . . . and it was quiet without the blonde's incessant muttering. Carla remembered the blonde, and shuddered.

She remembered Shapirro and the room with the black-and-white motif. Jordan. Dr. Arnaud. She hated them; it surged through her like power through a dynamo. It was the only thing that kept her brain active — all there was left to combat the insidious drug that sucked her vitality, draining her sanity.

If only Glenn would come . . . She knew she couldn't hang on much longer. A few more shots with the hypodermic and she would lose even her hatred. Then it would be too late. She'd become a plaything of the old man with white hair and pink eyes.

The click of the lock turning roused her. She struggled up through the grey mist, sat up in bed. The steel door opened and Glenn Waldemar came into the cell. Carla's heart thumped wildly — this was her chance.

Glenn closed the door behind him and dropped the key in his pocket. His oddly coloured eyes looked at Carla and he licked his lips.

His debonair manner left him; he was just an animal, wanting her. His voice was husky.

'You knew I'd be back, beautiful . . . and I am!'

Carla watched him stand his swordstick in the corner.

'Dr. Arnaud? Jordan?' she said. 'You're alone?'

Glenn Waldemar chuckled.

'The doctor is away, visiting our mutual friend Sylvester Shapirro. I gave Jordan a sleeping pill — he won't bother us!'

He pulled back the bedclothes and looked down at her. Glenn grabbed hold of her, his mouth was hot and passionate on hers, demanding kisses.

Carla pushed him off. She had to keep her head, stick to the plan she'd made. She said:

'Get this thing off my ankle — I can't make love while I'm chained.'

Glenn hesitated. He shrugged — she couldn't get away. He took another key from his pocket and unlocked the ankle band.

Carla tried not to show her exultation. He mustn't suspect what she had in mind. She held out her arms and said, softly:

'Glenn, I'm so lonely . . . and I love you, Glenn!'

Carla pulled him to her and kissed him. She let him get obsessed with her, waited till the last moment — till she had him under control. He was so taken by her beauty — he could think of nothing else.

Carla braced herself. She got her hands under his chest — and heaved. Glenn wasn't expecting anything like that. He rolled off the bed and crashed to the floor. He lay there, the breath knocked out of him.

Carla sprang off the bed and grabbed Glenn's swordstick. She twisted the handle till the six-inch steel blade shot out. She turned on Glenn Waldemar with a savage snarl.

'Scream,' she said. 'I want to hear you scream — go on! Dr. Arnaud is away. You drugged Jordan. We're alone — just you, and me! And now I'm going to pay you out for everything you've done to me . . . '

He backed away, scared. He saw the hatred blaze up inside her — knew she intended to kill him.

'Carla,' he sobbed, 'don't! I'll set you free — we'll go away together. We'll — '

She had him in a corner. He pressed back against the wall, trying to wriggle away. Carla brought the point of the steel level with his stomach. She leaned on it a little, drawing blood.

Glenn moaned: 'Don't! Carla — for God's sake . . . '

She leaned more heavily on the swordstick. The blade sank into his stomach, scraping his backbone. Tears rolled down Glenn's handsome face. Carla dug the blade in as far as it would go. She gripped the hilt tighter — twisted it cruelly.

Glenn shrieked. His hands went down to the stick and he tried to pull it out. He was losing strength fast. He slumped forward, unable to fall, pinned to the wall by the steel. Carla jerked the sword free. Glenn fell to the ground, moaning piteously, trying to stop the blood that pumped out of him, flooding the stone floor. Carla turned him over with her foot so that he lay on his back, staring up at her, shuddering.

His eyes were frightened. One frightened brown eye — one frightened blue eye. Carla selected the brown one. She placed the bloody tip of the steel blade to the pupil and thrust it home. Glenn screamed once — and stopped. The steel went into his brain and killed him instantly. Carla pulled the blade free and glared down at the corpse. She began to mutter to herself.

'Shapirro, you swine — your turn's coming . . . '

She went through Glenn Waldemar's pockets for keys. Unlocking the cell door, she went down the passage, the sword dripping blood in her hand. She unlocked the door at the end of the passage and went in search of Jordan.

She was thinking of how the male nurse had twisted her arms and hit her about the face while Dr. Arnaud shoved the needle in her arm. She was going to do something about Jordan.

He was slumped over a table, head down, sleeping. The glass of whisky Glenn had drugged lay shattered on the floor. Carla went in to him . . . when she came out there was fresh blood on the sword and Jordan wasn't going to wake up — ever.

Carla felt dizzy. She knew the dope was working on her. She had to get to Shapirro before she went under. She found some clothes and dressed hurriedly, stepping into a skirt, pulling a sweater over her head. She didn't bother with anything else. There was a redhead in another cell, drugged. Carla left her.

She went outside, gulping down clean fresh air. There was a car waiting, a black Rolls. Glenn's car, for which she had the keys. Carla got behind the wheel and drove off. She stopped at the first crossroads to study the signboard. It told her she was in Phoenix Springs. Clara headed for New York. Her lips set in a grim line.

Sylvester Shapirro was going to get his . . . but first, she wanted to see her father again. She drove furiously, heading for Mount Vernon and the home of Matthew Bowman.

★   ★   ★

He was cold. His bones seemed stiff, awkward to move. He did move, eventually — and moaned as the pain came back. So he lay still, thinking it out, trying to remember what had happened.

165

It came back slowly. His name was Eddie Gifford, and he was a private detective operating in New York City. So what was he doing lying in the road in the early morning?

Then it flooded back. The Waldemar twins. The killing at the *Paradise Club*. The chase to Phoenix Springs. Gringold and the patrolmen who beat him up. He began to wonder where the Rolls had gone, what had happened to the redhead. He felt sorry for her.

Again he tried to move. He straightened his legs, flexed his arms. Pain racked, him, and he lay still again. After a time, he began to feel his bones, gently. Nothing seemed broken . . . He forced himself to ignore the pain as he crouched, climbed upright. He lurched across to his car, fumbled for the whisky flask he kept in the dashboard locker.

He unscrewed the cap, and poured the raw liquid down his throat. His strength began to flow back. He emptied the flask and got behind the wheel. Fortunately the car had not been put out of commission. He started the engine and drove slowly along the road. He was in bad shape, in no condition for driving.

Eddie stuck at it, gritting his teeth. He had to get to a doctor — he knew that. He drove for seven miles before he saw a brass plate outside a bungalow. The plate said:

M. R. Brown, M.D.

Eddie stopped his car and got out. It was an effort to walk. He staggered drunkenly up the path and leaned on the door. His thumb found a bell push and he pushed it.

He kept his thumb on the button till he heard footsteps from inside.

An irate voice said: 'All right, all right — I'm coming!'

Then the door opened and Eddie fell forward into the doctor's arms. He passed out again.

When he came to, there was a strong smell of antiseptic in the air. He was lying in bed, covered in bandages. He could move, he discovered, without such intense pain now. Though he still felt weak. He remembered things more easily now.

It hit him suddenly. He had to do something in a hurry.

He started to get out of bed, shouted:

'Doc — you there?'

Dr. Brown came in. He frowned as he saw Eddie trying to walk.

'Get back to bed — you're not a fit man. You want to undo all my work?'

Eddie grinned weakly.

'Thanks for patching me up, doc. But there's a call I must make — right now. You got a phone?'

Dr. Brown made him sit on the bed while he brought the extension phone. Eddie got the operator and asked for the downtown Manhattan police precinct. He waited for the call to go through.

'Have I been out long, doc?' he asked.

'Nearly twelve hours. Is it that important?'

Eddie groaned, and jiggled the phone impatiently.

'I may be in time to stop a murder,' he said. 'And I may not!'

He was remembering that Gringold had been waiting for him. That meant

Shapirro knew who he was and why he was investigating — and Martha Franks lived alone in one room. He hoped he'd be in time.

A voice answered from Manhattan. Eddie said:

'Get down to Beckman Street in a hurry. There's an old lady, lives alone in 37a Gowan Mansions. There may be an attempt on her life.'

The voice that came back froze Eddie's blood.

'Too late, fellar . . . Mrs. Franks was battered to death last night!'

Eddie replaced the receiver. He looked at Dr. Brown and said:

'Too late!'

Eddie sat silent for a few minutes. He was thinking of Martha Franks and her husband. She'd told him to get Shapirro — well, he would. He stood up, trying out his legs and arms.

'If you think you're going any place,' Dr. Brown said, 'forget it. You'll fall flat on your face!'

Eddie shook his head.

'Sorry to walk out on you, doc. I know

169

you're right, but I've a job to do. Thanks for everything.'

He dressed, paid the doctor and promised he'd report to a hospital, and went out to his car. Dr. Brown watched him, sadly shaking his head. Eddie fumbled in the dashboard locker, bringing out a Luger and a package of shells . . .

He filled the magazine and slipped the gun in his pocket.

If anyone tried to stop him now, they were going to get hurt.

Eddie drove towards New York. He wasn't going fast, because he couldn't keep his foot hard on the accelerator.

And his arms were tired, pulling on the wheel. But he was moving towards the showdown. Shapirro wasn't going to get away with any more murders . . . he'd see to that. Personally.

He was keeping well into the right-hand curb and taking it steady. He didn't want any accidents just now. Suddenly, a car flashed by, heading the same way, towards the big city.

Eddie shot up, cursing. It was a black

Rolls! The glimpse he'd had of the driver revealed a girl with dark hair. Carla! Eddie decided it would be a good idea to call in at Mount Vernon and have a talk with her. Or her father. He tried to get a little more speed out of his car as he lost sight of the Rolls.

12

It didn't take Carla long to reach Mount Vernon. She swung into the drive leading up to her father's house, parked the Rolls and hurried up the steps to the door. She let herself in.

It was very quiet. Carla frowned; the butler should have been on duty, and he was nowhere to be seen. Perhaps he was with her father. She caught her breath — perhaps . . . no, *he* must be all right! She hurried up the stairs to her father's room and went in.

'Dad!' Carla gasped, ran across to the bed. She knew, even before she touched his cold, wrinkled skin, that he was dead. Tears came to her eyes; her breathing was heavy, choked. She buried her head in the sheets, kneeling by the bed, crying.

A harsh voice said: 'I thought you'd come back, Carla.'

She looked up at the tall figure of King Logan. His face was unshaven, his clothes dirty. He looked tired, hunted — and his eyes were cold and cruel as they bored into her.

'You!' she said. 'You killed him!'

King laughed.

'It was your fancy man, Shapirro — he told your father about you. I guess the old man just couldn't take it when he learnt what sort of a daughter he had!'

Carla blazed up.

'Shapirro! That swine — I'll — '

King struck her across the face, knocked her flat on the floor. He kicked her.

'Yeah, Carla,' he said, leering at her. 'I knew you'd come back if I waited. And now I'm going to finish you!'

Carla's mouth was dry. She was frightened.

'King — what is it? What's wrong?'

'Jerry was right,' King Logan spat. 'You are a double-crossing bitch! You sold out to Shapirro — ditched me for that skunk!'

'It isn't true,' Carla stormed. 'He kidnapped me. I've been beaten up, doped . . . I want to get Shapirro. We'll go after him together, King. You an' me, like old times.'

'I'm gonna shoot yuh where it hurts most,' he snarled. 'The soft lead will spread out inside yuh. You'll die slowly, painfully — the way double-crossers should die. And I'll sit here and watch, enjoying it, laughing . . . '

'No, King — no!'

Carla was sobbing, half with fright, half with rage. He couldn't kill her — not before she'd got Shapirro. But she knew he was going to.

She saw him point the gun at her stomach, leer at her.

'Now!' he said.

A shot thundered in the room. A stab of crimson flame — a puff of black smoke. A reek of cordite . . .

King Logan never pulled the trigger. He spun round as a lead slug crashed through his chest into his heart. Coughing blood He collapsed on the floor at her feet. The automatic dropped from his nerveless hand. He took about five seconds to die.

Carla looked at the man who had come into the room. He held a smoking Luger in his hand. He had curly brown hair and brown eyes and there was something about him that made Carla feel better. He was a decent sort of a guy.

He looked as if he'd taken a beating, his face was bruised and bandaged, and he walked stiffly, limping a little. He pulled her to her feet and said:

'Seems it was lucky for you I dropped in when I did. I suppose you're Carla Bowman — who was the boyfriend?'

His mouth had a quirk to it that might have been humorous once; now it was a grim line.

'King,' Carla said, staring at the corpse. 'King Logan.'

She wasn't seeing things clearly. The dope was still working inside her — and she hadn't yet got used to the idea that King was dead. Really dead. It was like living in a nightmare.

'So that was Logan,' said the man with the Luger. 'Well, it's no great loss to society. Maybe you found that out? Now tell me about Shapirro — I want to know everything about that guy.'

'Shapirro!' Carla's dark eyes blazed as she spat out the name. She seemed to come alive all at once. Her hands clenched in tight fists. 'I'm gonna get Shapirro — I'm gonna — '

He held her back.

'Take it easy, sister, take it easy. I'm the guy who's gonna take care of Sylvester Shapirro. He's my job!'

Carla looked at the man who had saved her life, She said:

'Who are you? How did you get here?'

Eddie Gifford told her. He told her about Martha Franks, about the Waldemar twins, the redhead who'd been kidnapped at the *Paradise Club*. About Gringold and the beating up he'd taken, about following her from Phoenix Springs.

Carla clenched her hands. Her face was a taut mask.

'Leave Shapirro to me, Eddie,' she said softly. 'I'm gonna take that swine apart!'

She started talking, fast. Telling him about Shapirro's harem; how she'd been taken to Dr. Arnaud's sanatorium and doped. Eddie wore a sympathetic expression by the time she'd finished.

'I guess you've had a tough time, baby. But that's over, now. You stay here and I'll get a doc to take a look at you. Meanwhile, I'll run out to the sanatorium and get the redhead; then I'll get the G-men and raid Shapirro's place.'

Eddie went out in a hurry. He had things to do.

★ ★ ★

Dr. Arnaud came into the room with the black glass walls. His face was white. Sylvester Shapirro pushed Phyllis away from him.

'I'll see you again, later,' he whispered.

The girl curtsied and left him. Arnaud blurted out:

'The game's up. Carla killed Glenn and Jordan, and got away. She's probably with the police now!'

Shapirro toyed with his whip. He scowled.

'What happened at the sanatorium?' he asked.

Dr. Arnaud had lost a lot of his briskness. He was nervous under Shapirro's pink eyes.

'I had to kill the redhead,' he said. 'I

couldn't leave her alive. I destroyed all the papers — there's nothing to link us with the place. Unless Carla talks!'

'Yes,' Shapirro whispered. 'Carla!' He brooded silently for a time. 'Will she be able to talk? How far was she under the drug?'

Arnaud shrugged helplessly.

'She was pretty far gone — but her resistance wasn't completely broken. She's out for revenge!'

'She must be killed — at once. Where's Rufus?'

Arnaud shuddered.

'He's gone stark mad. When he saw his brother's dead body, he went out — alone. He's gone after Carla. He'll never stop till he finds her . . . there was something between the twins. Like half of Rufus had been killed and the other half had to get the killer. He's crazy — berserk . . . '

Shapirro smiled.

'Let us hope,' he whispered, 'that Rufus finds her *before* she can open her mouth!'

He looked at the doctor and pressed a button on his desk.

'You've let me down, Arnaud,' he murmured. 'That's bad — you know what to expect.'

Dr. Arnaud took a step backwards.

'No — no!' he pleaded. 'It wasn't my fault — it was that fool, Jordan.'

The glass doors swung open and two hatchet men entered.

Shapirro said: 'I've finished with the doctor. Take him away!'

Arnaud whimpered.

'Don't kill me . . . don't — '

The two lean-faced killers grabbed his arms and hauled him towards the door. Shapirro sat at his transparent plastic desk, smiling, and listening to Arnaud's screams. The screams grew fainter as he was dragged down the staircase. He heard the muffled sound of a shot and the screams stopped. Dr. Arnaud had paid for his carelessness.

Sylvester Shapirro pressed another button on his desk.

'Come to your lord, Iris,' he whispered. 'He wants to nurse his baby . . . '

★ ★ ★

The chief of the local G-men was impressed by the way Eddie spoke. He listened carefully, refraining from interrupting.

'When I got to the sanatorium,' Eddie said, 'the redhead was dead. Her throat cut, very professionally — I guess Dr. Amaud used a scalpel on her. The private office was empty and there was a heap of ashes in the grate. Arnaud burnt all his papers before leaving . . . but that needn't stop you acting. Carla will confirm everything I told you.'

The G-man nodded.

'I've been waiting for this moment. Shapirro's been too clever for us to move before — but now, we'll take him!'

He snapped a switch and gave orders into a mike.

'Break out the arsenal. I want twenty men with tommy-guns in a hurry. Get the cars ready — we're raiding Shapirro's place at Montauk Point!'

Eddie smiled with satisfaction. Martha Franks was going to get her revenge after all.

The cars went out to Mount Vernon

first. The chief of the G-men wanted to see Carla. Eddie took him inside, where a puzzled doctor waited for them.

'I thought there was supposed to be a patient here,' the doc said. 'All I've found are two corpses. Old Bowman's, and a tall guy with a finger missing.'

'King Logan,' Eddie explained to the G-men. 'The girl, Carla? She was doped up to the eyebrows.'

The doctor shook his head.

'There's no girl here,' he said briefly.

Eddie cursed.

'We'd better hurry if we're gonna save Shapirro for the hot-seat. I guess Carla's gone gunning for him — and that dame means business!'

The G-men went back to their cars and set off for Montauk Point.

13

Where would she go? Where? *Where!*

The question drummed inside Rufus Waldemar's brain as he drove furiously towards New York. His grey suit was immaculate, his blond hair unruffled. Only his blue eyes registered the blazing fury of emotions inside him. They glinted like the sun on ice chips.

He'd lost his debonair manner now. His face was grim.

Carla — I'm coming for you, Carla! The thought drummed through his brain, obsessing him. He was going to kill her.

But she wasn't going to die quickly, easily. He was going to play with her first, make her scream, make her pray for death to come ... then, slowly, painfully ... he'd kill her as she'd killed his brother. He stroked his swordstick, smiling cruelly.

He remembered she'd lived with her father at Mount Vernon. And she was doped, incapable of going far. She might go to her father's house . . . she probably would.

Rufus Waldemar drove on for Mount Vernon, his handsome face a mask of insane desire, the desire to kill.

He reached Mount Vernon and swung his car into the drive. He saw a black Rolls parked outside the house.

Glenn's car! So she was here — his lips curled.

He braked his car and got out. He twisted the handle of his gold-tipped cane, admiring the cold steel blade that shot out. He went into the house.

Carla was coming down the stairs, dressed in the skirt and sweater she'd grabbed at the sanatorium. Her feet were still bare. They saw each other at the same time and Carla stopped dead in her tracks.

Rufus was glad she was beautiful. When he'd finished with her, no man would look at her face or figure without shuddering. He was going to carve her lovely body.

He went up the stairs towards her,

reaching out with the steel blade.

'You shouldn't have done it, Carla,' he said softly. 'You shouldn't have killed Glenn. Now I've got to kill you!'

Carla waited on the stairs. She didn't try to run. She might have been riveted to the spot with fear. She hadn't thought about Rufus, about the effect Glenn's death would have on him. She had only wanted to get at Sylvester Shapirro.

After Eddie had left, she'd thought about Shappiro, decided she was going after him herself. She didn't want anyone else to kill him — not after what he'd done to her. She wanted to kill him herself. So she'd picked up King's automatic and started down the stairs.

That's when she'd seen Rufus . . . and she still had the .45 in her hand. Rufus hadn't seen that. She waited for him to come closer . . . closer.

The sword almost touched her before she raised her hand. Rufus saw the automatic gleam in the light. He lunged forward, knowing he had to get her now. He was a fraction of a second too late.

Carla aimed at his chest and jerked the trigger.

The gun jumped in her hand. A .45 slug crashed into Rufus Waldemar's heart and he spun backwards, losing his foothold. He screamed as he fell, bumping on each step, all the way to the bottom. He lay in a heap, his limbs contorted, still. He was very dead.

Carla went down the stairs, gun in hand. She prodded the corpse with her bare foot, rolled it over. A red stain seeped through Waldemar's grey suit and his face had gone white. She passed him by, went out to the Rolls.

Shapirro! She was going after the old man with white hair, she was going to get him. She sat at the wheel of the car, thinking. There were certain practical considerations, such as: how was she going to get at him?

There was a high wall round the house at Montauk Point; a steel door, guarded by armed men; fierce dogs patrolled the grounds. She had Waldemar's car. Would that be allowed through the gate without question? Not with her at the wheel. But with Rufus Waldemar . . .

She went back to the house and dragged the corpse out to the car. She propped it on the seat next to the wheel, fixing it so it wouldn't roll sideways. She got in and drove off. The guards weren't to look closely at Rufus Waldemar — they weren't going to know he was dead at all. They were going to let him in through the gates . . . and that was all she wanted.

The dope had made her a little crazy. No one but a crazy woman would have driven out to Montauk Point with a corpse and a .45 to beard Shapirro in his den. But Carla was past worrying about the odds against her. She knew she wasn't going to recover from the treatment she'd had; knew the dope had a hold on her for all time. All she thought about now was revenge.

Then she saw the vast, rambling house on the cliff edge, heard the Atlantic rollers pound on the rocks. Carla drove right up to the gate. She drove with one hand on the wheel, the other gripping King's automatic. She was ready to stop any argument with flying lead.

The steel gate opened. A guard glanced at the car. He saw Waldemar and a dame, nothing unusual in that. He waved them in.

She got out of the car and went into the house, gun in hand. She passed through the deserted hallway with its black and white tiles to the staircase that spiraled upwards to Shapirro's room. She padded softly along the balcony with its black jade and silver statuettes, drew back the dark drapes and pushed open the glass doors.

Carla stepped into the fantastic room with the black glass walls, her automatic ready to blast Shapirro at his desk. But the room was empty.

Concealed lighting illumed the jet-black ceiling, the tiled floor. She saw the whip lying on the transparent plastic desk, smelt the heavy aroma of burning incense. Carla swore. She had fully expected Shapirro to be there . . . now she would have to wait for him to return. He couldn't be far — he never left the house.

And when he did come back, he might

have his hatchet men with him. Carla wanted him alone. She looked round for a hiding place. The glass walls were bare; the furniture clear plastic. There was nowhere she could hide — unless . . .

She saw the black coffin with its silver nameplate: KING LOGAN. Carla smiled. King wasn't going to need that just yet. She threw back the lid and stared into the dark interior. It was just the place to hide; Shapirro wasn't going to look for anyone in a coffin. She climbed inside and lowered the lid. Shapirro was due for a shock when he returned. She laughed softly as she lay flat, thinking . . . a coffin for Carla!

★　★　★

Darkness was creeping across Long Island as the cars carrying the G-men rushed northwards to Montauk Point. The rising moon cast a pale light over the countryside, turning the broad concrete strip into a silver lane between ghostly trees.

Eddie sat next to the chief of the

G-men in the leading car. He felt the bulge of the Luger in his pocket and knew he would use it before the night was over. He was tensed up, ready for action and sudden death. This was the showdown.

As the car swooped on, Eddie thought back over the trail of violence that had caught him up in its hideous mesh . . . King Logan and his gang carrying on a protection racket in the Bowery; Carla, the society girl who wanted thrills — she'd got them all right. More than she bargained for.

Shapirro cutting in on Logan; his twin killers, the Waldemars. Old Matthew Bowman whose heart couldn't take the truth about his daughter. Piggot, the detective whose body had been fished out of the Hudson.

Then Carla had gone to Shapirro, ratted on King. She'd realized her mistake too late. After she'd seen him, seen for herself how he treated his girls. Doped them, used them as playthings for his unnatural desires. Too late, she'd tried to back out. Shapirro had doped her, sent her to Dr. Arnaud's sanatorium at

Phoenix Springs for treatment. She'd had a rough time all right.

Eddie's face tightened into grim lines. Martha's death had affected him more than any of the others. Shapirro was going to pay for that — Eddie would see to it, personally.

Carla had escaped, killed Glenn and the male nurse. He shuddered as he imagined the scene; Carla making love to Glenn, leading him on to his death. King Logan was dead, too. Eddie had shot him at Mount Vernon, saving Carla's life. He couldn't think why he'd bothered . . . she wasn't worth saving. A gang-leader's moll who didn't stop at murder herself.

Eddie had been too late arriving at the sanatorium — the birds had flown. But this time, they wouldn't be too late. No one was going to escape from the house at Montauk Point. No one.

He wondered if Carla had got into the house. She was after Shapirro and, doped as she was, she wasn't going to be stopped easily. She wanted her revenge — but the house was guarded by armed thugs. Carla might well be dead at that moment. But if she wasn't . . . despite himself, Eddie felt pity for Shapirro. He wasn't going to die pleasantly if Carla got her hands on him.

The cars tore on into the night. The G-man said:

'Ten minutes now — then we'll see some action!'

'I keep thinking of those crooked cops at Phoenix Springs,' Eddie said. 'Gringold and Louis and Buck. I'd like to meet up with them again, after this show is over.'

The G-man smiled mirthlessly.

'Don't worry about them. Gringold won't be a chief of police after I make my report to Washington. A lot of Shapirro's yes-men down at the City Hall are going to wish they hadn't covered up for him too.'

The cars were out in the open, following the road that wound across sandy dunes. The sea wasn't far away: Eddie could hear the Atlantic breakers in the distance. Then he saw the house on the rise.

'That's it,' the G-man said. 'Montauk Point — Shapirro's fortress!'

He signalled, and the cars stopped a little way from the house. Twenty determined and well-trained men lined up to take their orders. Twenty men armed with tommy-guns, ready to fight for the right of ordinary people to live in peace.

'We're going straight in,' said the chief of the G-men. 'We want Shapirro, the kingpin of the outfit. His mobsters will try to stop you. Remember, this isn't a picnic — shoot to kill! That's all.'

They moved in on the house. Four rope ladders, with steel hooks, were slung over the high wall. The G-men swarmed up, and over. Eddie dropped to the ground on the inside and looked around him.

There was a sudden cry. The guards had seen them!

Instantly, shots rang out. Crimson flame stabbed the darkness. A hail of lead slugs poured through the trees. A G-man fell to the ground, riddled with bullets.

Eddie dived for cover, cursing. This meant that Shapirro would be warned — almost certainly, he would have a line of retreat prepared. He started running forward, dodging from tree to tree, firing all the time.

The guards had moved back from the steel gates, machine-guns chattering viciously. The air was acrid with cordite fumes, bright with the stabbing flames of gunfire. Deep-throated dogs bayed and plunged through the trees.

Eddie tripped on a trailing rambler and fell headlong. A dog pounced on him. A large fierce animal, with bloodshot eyes and savage teeth. It lashed him with sharp claws, ripping his clothes. Eddie rolled over, keeping his arm over his face. The dog was a killer, trained to take life. To rip out a victim's eyes, gouge his throat.

Eddie gasped for breath and tried to get his Luger under the animal's body. Its breath was hot on his face; its claws left bleeding weals on his flesh. It tried to sink its teeth into his throat. Eddie pushed the barrel of his Luger into its great body and fired. The dog rolled off him, twitched convulsively, and lay still.

Another brute sprang at him. Eddie jerked the trigger, placing a slug between its red eyes. It died in mid-air, crashed at his feet. Eddie, panting, wiped blood from his face and lurched behind a tree as a hail of machine-gun fire blasted in his direction.

He saw the would-be killer, lean and hatchet-faced, sheltering behind a fir tree. Eddie snapped a shot, winged him. The machine-gun stopped abruptly and Eddie dashed forward again, keeping under cover, moving nearer the house.

He glimpsed three G-men, flat on their stomachs, firing into a copse. A grenade landed in their midst, exploded, blew them to small shreds. Eddie saw the bomb-thrower dodge through the trees. He aimed, fired. The slug caught the killer low down, in the kidneys. The man rolled on the ground, writhing, moaning.

He heard the chief of the G-men shout:

'Get into the house! Get Shapirro!'

Eddie plunged on, recklessly. Shapirro might be getting away under cover of the gunfight. He could easily lose himself in the confusion. A barrage of lead ripped long furrows in the soft earth at Eddie's feet. He threw himself sideways, firing back. His Luger stopped suddenly; the hammer thudding on an empty chamber. Cursing, Eddie ran for cover, shoving a new magazine in place as he ran.

Gunfire was sporadic now. The G-men had wiped out most of the opposition. They started grimly forward, determined to take the fortress. New reinforcements came out of the house.

A sharpshooter with a rifle fitted with telescopic sights shot down two G-men in cold blood before Eddie got him. Another grenade exploded, close by. The blast lifted Eddie off his feet, threw him into a bush.

He picked himself up, dazed, and went on again. Another dog hurled itself at him. Eddie dropped to one knee, steadied his hand, fired. The weight of the dead body landing on him knocked him backwards. Machine-gun fire blasted from the veranda of the house, sending G-men sprinting for cover.

Someone was moving near Eddie. Friend or Foe? He glimpsed a hatchet face, an upraised arm. The mobster snarled and leapt at Eddie, knife in hand.

The steel blade glinted in the moonlight, flashed as it came down in a vicious arc. Eddie fell backwards, hitting the ground with a thud. The knife buried itself in the earth, an inch from his ear.

Eddie brought up his knee as the killer came down on top of him. He caught the hatchet man full in the stomach winding him. Eddie threw the man away from him, brought round his Luger, blasted him with a heavy slug.

They were nearly to the house now. Eight G-men had fallen; the others pressed on, shooting their way through Shapirro's gunmen. Eddie caught up with them, joined in the battle. The lead started flying again. Shapirro's mob had good concealment behind the stonework of the veranda. They took advantage of it, blazing away with their tommy-guns.

The G-men were going in. They broke cover, raced across the open ground, firing continuously. Two of them dropped in their tracks. The others reached the veranda engaged the mobsters in pitched battle. The walls of the house reverberated with gunfire.

Eddie stumbled on a corpse, stopped to grab a machine-gun. He climbed on the veranda spraying lead into the hatchet men grouped about the door of the house. They scattered. Eddie and the G-men went after them, through the wide doors, into Shapirro's fortress.

Eddie had no time to marvel at Shapirro's choice of interior decoration. He had an impression of black and white, sombre lighting, and a spiral staircase that swept up to a balcony. Then the lead was flying again. Blood and dead bodies covered the black and white tiles. Shapirro's mob was desperate. They knew they'd go to the electric chair if they were taken — so they fought to a finish. Like rats cornered, they snarled and spat and shot down the G-men.

But Eddie and the G-men were not going to be stopped, not now. Guns blazing, they swept forward, shooting their way to the bottom of the stairs. The half-dozen remaining hatchet men retreated upwards, exchanging shots with the G-men below.

The G-men concentrated their fire

— poured a deadly hail of lead up the staircase, driving the mobsters back. The spiral stairs were empty except for the dead. From the balcony, the last of Shapirro's mob fired back; then he too, fled.

It was silent for a moment. Eddie raced up the stairs, lips tight, eyes cold. His gun was levelled and he was thinking of Sylvester Shapirro. Suddenly, fresh shots echoed from a room on the balcony. Eddie's legs moved quicker. Again he remembered Carla. A burst of machine-gun fire was followed by a brief silence — then came a single shot. And silence.

Eddie pushed back the black drapes and passed through swinging glass doors to a fantastic room with black glass.

He knew, then, that he was too late.

14

It was dark, dark and hot and stifling inside the coffin. Fortunately, King had been a tall, broad man so Carla wasn't cramped for space. She had room to move her legs, to wriggle into a more comfortable position.

She had no idea how long she'd been lying in the coffin in the room with black glass walls, waiting for Sylvester Shapirro to return. It seemed like hours; probably, it was only minutes.

She lifted the lid an inch and wedged the barrel of her automatic between the side of the box and the lid. It gave her a slit to watch though, let some air in. Air scented with incense. Carla watched and waited.

She heard footsteps, tensed expectantly. The glass doors swung open and Shapirro and three hatchet men came into the room. Carla didn't move. She could have shot down Shapirro where he stood, but she didn't want him to die that easily. She wanted to get him alone, to play with him a little before she killed him.

She hoped the hatchet men would go away soon. She knew the dope running through her veins was becoming more active, dulling her brain, reducing her steadily to the level of an automaton. She'd have to deal with Shapirro very soon, or it would be too late. She lay in the coffin, watching Shapirro through the slit she'd wedged with her gun barrel.

Shapirro was excited about something. He moved restlessly about the room, cracking his long whip, jerking his head. His mop of snow-white hair danced and his pink eyes gleamed in a strange manner. He said:

'Rufus dead! You say Carla was with him when he came through the gate? The fools! They should have known better than to let her in.'

'We've combed the house and gardens. There's no trace of her anywhere.'

Carla smiled coldly and tightened her finger round the trigger of her .45.

Shapirro didn't know how close he was to death.

Shapirro said: 'Turn the dogs loose. Search the gardens again. Post men at all entrances to the house. She must be found!'

Two of the hatchet men left the room. The third stayed on. Carla was tempted to shoot him, then deal with Shapirro.

She controlled her excitement, decided to wait a little longer.

Shapirro went to his desk and sat down. She could see the lines of dissipation on his chalk-white face, the pouches under his eyes. He suddenly looked very old. He was frightened. He knew he had a crazy woman in the house, a girl doped till she had only hatred and revenge left in her. And he was scared.

He whispered, and the sound crept eerily round the room, echoing from the black glass walls:

'She must be killed!'

Carla enjoyed lying there, watching him, knowing she could end his life at any second — watching him shake with fear. Fear that she was near — and out to get him. It pleased her that he knew she was so close — yet not knowing exactly how close!

Sylvester Shapirro stroked the lash of his whip and whispered: 'Carla *must* die!'

The hatchet man glanced round the room. His sharp eyes passed over the glass walls, the transparent furniture. He ignored the coffin . . .

'One thing, boss,' he said. 'She ain't in here!'

Carla amused herself by training the muzzle of her gun on Shapirro's face, shifting it from one pink eye to the other. She could kill him any time she wanted . . . it was as much as she could do to stop the mad laughter bursting from her lips.

Suddenly, abruptly, there came the sound of shots. Bursts of machine-gun fire from the grounds outside. Shapirro grabbed a telephone and snapped into it:

'What's going on out there? Have you found the girl? What . . . ? What! The cops . . . '

He listened for long seconds, slammed down the phone. His face was haggard when he looked at the hatchet man.

'G-men have surrounded the house. They're attacking in force, with tommy-guns. And Eddie Gifford is with them!'

'G-men!' snarled the mobster. 'Lousy — swine!'

Shapirro calmed himself.

'We've time to get away,' he whispered. 'Go downstairs and organize the defence. The G-men must be kept out of the house till I've had time to arrange matters.'

His face took on a ruthless expression.

'The girls,' he said, 'they can't be allowed to live. I'll deal with them myself. And there are papers I must burn. Tell Nansen to prepare the launch for a getaway by sea.'

The hatchet man hurried out of the room, leaving Shapirro alone — with Carla!

Carla eased up the lid of the coffin, very quietly. Shapirro had his back to her. She climbed out of the box, crept up on him, gun in hand. Eddie's arrival with the G-men gave her the chance she'd been waiting for. Shapirro's mob would be busy fighting — and she had the old man with white hair and pink eyes all to herself.

Shapirro pressed a button on his desk and a section of the glass wall became transparent. He stared at the lovely girls who posed for his amusement . . . his harem. It would be the last time he'd ever enjoy their exquisite forms, their fancy dresses. He couldn't let them live — not now.

Carla hissed: 'Move away from the desk Shapirro — don't touch any of those push buttons or I'll blow your head off!'

Sylvester Shapirro turned in his seat. He saw Carla, in a skirt and sweater, glaring at him with a maniacal light in her jet-black eyes, her finger curling threateningly round the trigger of a .45 automatic. He slid out of his seat, away from the desk.

Carla laughed softly. It wasn't a pleasant sound. Shapirro shuddered. He knew enough of insanity to recognize it when he saw it. And he saw it now — staring at him out of Carla's eyes.

'This is it, Shapirro,' she said. 'The end

— for you! No more doped girls to play with — I'm going to feed you to the worms!'

He backed away from her, slowly. He was ageing fast, sweating with fear. He croaked:

'Carla, my dear — my beautiful Carla — put that gun down and we'll go away together. In my launch, far away . . . '

She smiled. The sort of smile death wears.

'You forget I'm full of dope,' she said. 'I wouldn't live long . . . long enough to become one of your toys, then — '

'There's an antidote,' he whispered. 'I'll give it to you. You're too lovely to die, Carla.'

He was looking at her body, his pink eyes caressing her slender legs and tapering thighs. Even now, his mind couldn't keep off her beauty.

'You think I'd trust you?' Carla played with him, let him hope she might fall under his spell. 'After what you've done to me?'

The sound of gunfire was louder now. The G-men were closing in on the house.

Carla wasn't going to leave him for them to deal with. When Eddie arrived, Shapirro was going to be beyond help.

She took his whip off the desk and cracked it in the air.

'You know what I'm going to do?' she said softly. 'I'm going to whip you — give you a taste of your own medicine. Only, I shan't be playing . . . I'm going to whip the life out of you!'

She lashed out, struck him across the face. The whip came away with skin on the tip . . . Shapirro moaned and staggered back, holding his hands to his bleeding face. Carla slashed him again and again, striking his hands, reducing them to a pulp. His arms fell to his sides and Carla lashed his face till it was raw. Blood poured down over his white shirt, his black suit. Shapirro screamed with agony.

Carla laughed. Her peals of laughter shook the room, echoed eerily from the walls. Mad, crazy laughter of an insane person. She felt the dope course through her veins, felt hatred surge up inside her. This was the man — this . . . swine!

— who'd filled her full of dope.

Carla wheeled towards the glass wall of the harem.

'See?' she cried. 'Your lord cowers in fear! Watch him shrink from the lash — hear him scream. He's paying for what he did to you . . . '

The doped girls in ridiculous costumes stared blindly, seeing it all and not showing the slightest sign of emotion. They were past understanding. Will-less zombies who had lost even the desire for revenge.

Carla flayed Shapirro as he huddled at her feet. The lash broke through his flesh, touched a nerve. Carla concentrated on it. Again and again, the whip stung the same nerve, driving him mad with excruciating pain. Shapirro shrieked like a lost soul in hell.

Shapirro tried to crawl away from the stinging lash. Carla pursued him round the room, leaving a trail of blood across the black-and-white tiles.

'I hid in the coffin, Shapirro — you never thought of that, did you? King's coffin! I was there all the time, waiting for you!'

Shapirro might not have heard her. He huddled in a heap on the floor, whimpering, hardly trying to keep off the cruel lash. His pink eyes were bloodshot, weeping continuous tears. His hair and face and hands were plastered with blood, stained a dark red. He lay in a pool of his own blood, staring up at Carla like a dog begging its master to stop beating it. He was no longer capable of coherent speech.

'You killed my father, you swine!' Carla grated. 'The only person I cared for. He had a weak heart and you told him about me and King . . . murdered him with cruel words.'

She went on whipping him. Sweat poured down her face; her shoulders heaved with the effort. Her raven-black hair straggled down over her eyes — she pushed it back with the gun she still held in her other hand.

'You've lost your fancy ways now, haven't you?' she jeered. 'You're not thinking of the girls in the next room now, are you? Phyllis, in her gym tunic — Iris, with her diaper! And the others . . . '

Shapirro moaned with new agony. His moans turned to agonized screams as she bared a fresh nerve centre. Carla let him taste the whip again. He was dying, she knew that.

Outside, the gunfire was much closer. It sounded right outside the walls of the house, on the veranda. A grenade exploded somewhere. Carla wondered how much longer she had before Eddie arrived.

She smashed the glass wall separating the harem, and cried:

'Look at him cringe! Your lord is dying . . . '

The doped girls stared helplessly, unmoving. If they knew what was happening, they didn't show it. If they enjoyed watching Shapirro get his deserts, no one would have known from their expressionless faces. They went on posing, the way they'd been trained.

Carla paused, gasping for air. Her exertions were beginning to tire her. The dope seemed to be taking a more vicious hold on her. She felt weak. Her head swam and the grey mist started to come back. The room began to blur.

The black glass walls seemed to recede from her. She felt herself falling . . . there was a dark tunnel opening to engulf her. Carla clung to her hatred, dragged herself up out of the grey mist. She attacked Shapirro again.

'You killed my father,' she whispered venomously. 'You murdered him!'

She said it over and over, as if she were in a trance — like the blonde who'd been in her cell at the sanatorium in Phoenix Springs. Her mind was going — snapping. She had almost exhausted her reserves of strength. The hatred that had kept her going was rapidly being used up. Shapirro was dying at her hand, before her eyes, and she no longer had an anchor to keep her in the world of the living.

Carla went after Shapirro again. He had stopped crawling now, and lay in a heap, moaning softly. He looked more like an animal than a man. His clothes were almost gone, whipped to shreds. His flesh was a raw mass of red weals. There was hardly an inch of white skin left on him; Carla's insane laughter pealed through the room, echoed off the black glass walls. She knew she was crazy, beyond the help of any doctor. The dope had done its work too well. A white froth bubbled at her crimson lips as she lashed Shapirro. She laughed till the tears rolled down her lovely cheeks, till her whole body shook and quivered.

The grey mist came back to engulf her. She felt herself being sucked down. This was the end — she knew it as surely as she knew she must finish Shapirro in her last few seconds of consciousness. The whip fell from her shaking hand.

She raised the automatic, aimed it unsteadily at the heap of flesh on the floor. She fired three times, reeling back as the gun exploded flame and lead in her hand. The .45 slugs tore into Shapirro's heart and he stopped moaning, stopped writhing. Sylvester Shapirro was dead — dead as his innocent victims.

Gunfire on the balcony outside made Carla turn. She saw the glass doors swing open and the last of Shapirro's hatchet men come in. He saw Carla, the dead body of Shapirro, and snarled. His tommy-gun sprayed lead slugs across the room.

Carla spun round as the stream of lead hit her. The bullets ripped into her dark flesh, tearing the life out of her.

She saw the figure of the hatchet man loom above her, a vague blur in the mist that darkened everything about her.

She jerked the trigger of her automatic, blasted a single shot at him. The last thing she was aware of was his falling body. Then she blacked out . . . knew nothing more.

Eddie Gifford came through the glass doors in a hurry. He saw Carla, sprawled under the body of the hatchet man. They were both dead. Then he saw the heap of raw flesh in the corner, and the bloody lash. He had to guess it was Sylvester Shapirro — he had to guess, even, that it had once been a man at all.

He felt sick in his stomach. Carla had got Shapirro, the way she said she would. He tried not to feel sorry for the man who had killed Martha. But, looking at the mess Carla had made of him, it was difficult.

He stood silent, looking round the fantastic room. He saw the doped girls, motionless, their faces blank. He didn't know if they were aware that their tormentor was dead. He couldn't face their blindly staring eyes; he looked quickly away.

Martha was avenged. All the people Shapirro had murdered were avenged. His job was over. He could walk out of the house at Montauk Point and drive back to New York. He could get drunk and try to forget this hideous room. He could try — but he knew he'd never really forget it. The scene was indelibly engraved on his mind for all time.

Eddie looked at Carla. She suddenly seemed very young; a lovely, innocent girl who'd been caught up in the meshes of violence and bloodshed. Trapped by the pseudo-glamour of the gangster's way of life. His eyes caught sight of the black coffin with the silver nameplate: KING LOGAN. Carla had been King's moll . . . it seemed appropriate that she should have her lover's coffin. He picked up her limp body and carried it across to the alcove and laid her flat in the bottom of the black box and closed the lid.

He turned away, thinking of Martha . . . and Old Matthew Bowman. Yeah, it was appropriate . . . *A coffin for Carla!*

THE END

We do hope that you have enjoyed reading this large print book.

Did you know that all of our titles are available for purchase?

We publish a wide range of high quality large print books including:
Romances, Mysteries, Classics
General Fiction
Non Fiction and Westerns

Special interest titles available in large print are:
The Little Oxford Dictionary
Music Book, Song Book
Hymn Book, Service Book

Also available from us courtesy of Oxford University Press:
Young Readers' Dictionary
(large print edition)
Young Readers' Thesaurus
(large print edition)

For further information or a free brochure, please contact us at:
Ulverscroft Large Print Books Ltd.,
The Green, Bradgate Road, Anstey,
Leicester, LE7 7FU, England.
Tel: (00 44) 0116 236 4325
Fax: (00 44) 0116 234 0205

Her Majesty's Secret Service agent Garrett, investigating a series of suicides by scientific researchers, discovers the parameters of a cataclysmic terrorist strike. The fanatical André Dur puts his unholy scenario into operation over the geological fault called the 'Rat Run', where nuclear submarines stalk each other in the dark depths. Helplessly the world looks on as the minutes tick away. Garrett's desperate mission is to neutralise Dur's deadly countdown — the ultimate ecological disaster, Chernobyl on the high seas.

THE SECRET AGENT

Rafe McGregor

Two days after September 11, 2001, an intelligence officer from the South African Secret Service arrived in Washington, D.C. Three months later he was responsible for the arrest of Richard Reid, the notorious British *al-Qaeda* operative . . . A series of short stories follow secret agent Jackson from Boston to Oxford, Quebec City, the Italian Alps, and his final and most deadly mission four months after his premature retirement.

THE PRICE OF FREEDOM

E. C. Tubb

When his wife is murdered, the victim of an assassin's bullet, businessman Dell Weston soon finds his life is falling apart. Betrayed by his partner, he loses control of his company, and descends into the lower strata of a dog-eat-dog society. Somehow, Dell manages to survive long enough to question the very fabric of civilisation — and the role played by the mysterious figures in grey — the Arbitrators . . .